WHERE YOU ARE

Stories
by
Randy Kraft

Library of Congress Control #2025914767
Published in the United States
September 2025
ISBN #978-0-9973791-5-0
www.maple57press.com

These stories are works of fiction.
Any similarity to real persons is coincidence.
AI was not used in the writing.

Cover photograph by Jacques Garnier
from his *Estero* series
www.jacques-garnier.com

Cover Design by David Smith
www.designdsmith.com

Also by Randy Kraft
OFF SEASON
RATIONAL WOMEN [Stories]
SIGNS OF LIFE
COLORS OF THE WHEEL

www.randykraftwriter.com

*How happy life would be if an undertaking retained
to the end the delight of its beginning, if the dregs of
a cup of wine were as sweet as the first sip.*
W. Somerset Maugham

*In old age we should wish still to have passions
strong enough to prevent us turning on ourselves.*
Simone de Beauvoir

*But you know that when the truth is told, that you
can get what you want or you can just get old.*
Billy Joel

Locked in at the Inn

I walk around topless these days, something I would never have dreamed of doing most of my life, to the chagrin of my husbands. Like many of my generation, I was indoctrinated to modesty, trained to dress properly, meaning conceal the so-called private parts. Sensuality, with all its erotic secrets, reserved for behind closed doors, and only for the deserving. Over time, frankly, a long time, abetted by feminist rhetoric and spirited literary heroines, I have finally realized that rules restraining our true selves serve no good purpose, not even for those of us who believe in playing by the rules.

Thus, to the delight of my current, and likely last lover, Robert, I've liberated my inner tramp. As much as I despise the misogyny in that word, I applaud the dominion. I'd so much rather choose than be chosen.

Never too late for anything is the better mantra at any stage of life.

In my youth, I had a firm body, slim and trim, it was said, and now, in my late sixties, still so, although, perky breasts have gone the way of sails in slack wind and my derriere is decidedly flatter. Rob doesn't mind. My body rises to his touch, which is all a man of seventy needs. He may have fantasies not yet revealed. Time will tell. The life we're living is fantasy enough for me, and he says he's grateful to be sleeping with a woman of substance. Strolling about half-naked, a bonus.

We moved last year to a late 19th century estate purchased by Rob's brother, Fred. Once a grand chateau spread over an expansive land parcel on what is called the North Fork of Long Island, a sweeping Gatsbyesque lawn faces a tidal estuary formed by rivers from New York and New England, and the Long Island Sound leading to the Atlantic. The towns on this tine are the less populated and less glitzy of the two-pronged island, which is actually a sliver of land. At its tip, a ferry landing, to and from Connecticut, faces the tony Shelter Island and privately owned Gardiner Island. I had no idea islands are subject to ownership and I suspect Fred, a retired hedge fund guru, the type the novelist Tom Wolfe branded a *master of the universe,* would like one of his own. Rebuilding this estate must have been his Plan B, and for

Rob, a late life diversion after a lifelong career as a neurosurgeon.

The two spent three years planning and overseeing the renovation of this oversized, overwrought homage to wealthy industrialists into a first class vacation retreat for their 21st century equivalents. They picked it up for a song, Rob said, because it was in shambles, trapped for decades in the sort of trust dispute legendary among such elites. Working with an expert in restoration and a fashionable, high-priced interior designer, they converted this weary matron from disheveled to refined. Reminds me of a Damon Runyon depression-era tale in which a beggar is transformed into an elegant doyenne to ensure her daughter's marriage to royalty. In that tale, however, the rehabilitation was made possible by a scrappy bunch of bootleggers, rather than retirees with time and money to burn.

And then, just as the finishing touches were in sight, the pandemic lockdown sent everyone scrambling like bats in daylight, and the hospitality trade collapsed. So, the three of us decided to camp out at this classy hideout.

Two old men and an old lady displaced in time and space – fable or gothic novel?

Fred occupies the west wing and we, the east, so I greet the sunrise with the delight of each new day. We meet at midday, most days, driven by the solar arc toward the kitchen, dead center of the property, opening to a terrace on the south side facing the water, where I often sunbathe topless. I'm sure I've seen Fred peek, but he keeps a proper distance.

Because he frequently cites the Middle Eastern and European capitals where he has business interests, I've often wondered if Fred was a spy. He has a le Carrê sort of personality. He rarely makes eye contact, his expression ranges from somber to scowling, he's pensive, an observer, slithering about like a lizard searching for shade. Maybe he has great stories to tell, if pressed to reveal, like W. Somerset Maugham, a prolific storyteller, who was a real secret agent and published his tales after the fact. Maybe Fred might be urged to fess up. After all, our secrets define us, although among men buttoned up so tight, maybe hard to crack.

During the summer of the lockdown, I reclined afternoons on one of the two chaises left out by the sapphire blue-tiled infinity pool, sipping the lemonade I pitcher every morning. I closed my eyes to isolate the sound of water lapping toward the shoreline, as I might tune out percussion in a classic music piece, in favor of strings. Birds gregariously warbled sweet arias, freed from man-made noise dimmed by global house arrest. Lavender perfume from a nearby field floated over my resting body on a gentle breeze, and I pictured a parade of ants restoring the earth below me, while I, their queen, in effect, served as sentinel.

I don't imagine any future guests will appreciate this idyl as much as I have.

The pool is punctuated at one end by a square jacuzzi, room for eight, abutting a large, also square lily pond. When I proposed adding koi to the pond, Fred smirked, but then, struck by the marketing lightbulb, cried, *we could fill it with Garrarufan! You know, those tiny fish that nibble at the skin, like at a Swiss spa.*

They starve those fish, the Garrarufan, so they are reduced to nibbling on dead skin cells for nourishment, I pronounced, having read this in *National Geographic. As a rule,* I hastened to add, before he had the chance to insert a patronizing remark, *they thrive on plankton and plant sources indigenous to the waters of the Middle East, their native territory.*

Rob smiled with pride, delighted at my

willingness to tangle with his big brother, as he tends to be deferential.

A well-documented health risk, Rob stated. *We would not want our guests to think we do not have their best interests at heart.*

Nor to be cruel to any living creatures, I could not help but add, as punctuation.

And then, surprisingly, we all laughed. A rare moment of shared hilarity. Most of the time, we tiptoed around each other, navigating in our own lanes to avoid collision of spirit or individuality, something I mastered during my second marriage because that husband was hot tempered. Sexy and smart, but hypersensitive.

Fred manages planning and operations, while Rob will be, as he describes it, the front man. He told me, when he suggested we move to the chateau, that his brother had tired of the burden of the business that made him and his clients wealthy. Tired of the responsibility for investors and his team, he said, not to mention the histrionic vicissitudes of a global economy, finance having no aim other than to create finance, the means the end. To my mind, an incredible bore, beyond the burden.

The truth is, I think he was in it for the prestige more than the money, Rob speculated.

And were you a surgeon for the prestige? I inquired.

We were seated at a candlelit corner table in a café at the time, pre-lockdown, knees touching and the conversation flirtatious.

Somewhat, I suppose, although medicine is more of a calling, he answered, with a smile.

Rob may be self-righteous, as surgeons can be, but he is not a man of false fronts. And, he has a wonderfully seductive smile.

So what will be prestigious about being an innkeeper? I felt compelled to ask.

He chuckled. *I guess I'll find out.*

I believe Fred liked the idea of being the master of a tangible realm, and Rob liked the idea of being useful, particularly to his brother. He is the more thoughtful of the two, if equally intense. When he retired, tired of his burden of godly intervention, he found himself aimless, he said, until Fred suggested this project.

You might say they were both masters of their universes. Me too, in a small way. After forty years teaching high school English, you might say I once aimed to master fertile minds.

Before all this, the three of us, like most of our contemporaries, expected to enjoy our waning years not quite irresponsibly, rather responsible to ourselves. No longer to clients or patients, students or administrators, or loved ones for that matter, although high achieving baby boomers like us take our obligations to others quite seriously. We cannot shed that disposition like dry skin.

Wandering the grounds has been a form of therapy for me, dressed or otherwise. I also meander from room to room among the five on our wing, decorated in what I would describe as new millennium Edith Wharton. Reclaimed mixed wood flooring, like Fir, Maple, Hickory, are native to Long Island. Stone counters evoke an earthiness the affluent crave. Plush king-size beds are crowned with headboards upholstered in burgundy or ochre, and dressed in stark white Egyptian cotton. Recycled wine barrels from local vineyards were reconfigured into bedstands, chargers deftly hidden within. Gleaming glamorous bathrooms are anchored by oversized showers, with sunken hot tubs for two on private patios, accessed by glass doors that fold fully into frames like magic, sheltered by graceful weeping willows.

Staged serenity for guests suffering an interior chaos they will not or cannot dispel.

Fred's wing is comparable in dimension

and room count, of course, and between us, off the terrace, a dining area and a chef's kitchen, still sparkling, because we have either ordered foods in or maneuvered in one tight corner of the kitchen, like squatters, which we clean up so thoroughly every evening, one might never know we were there.

Then again, when the Sound Inn at last opens, I'll have to cover up. And they will have to hire staff, which was precluded by the virus.

None of us supposed it would be over a year before travelers tentatively ventured out, and it was only because Fred managed their investments well, and the equity markets were surprisingly resilient, they were able to pay taxes and construction loans, and retain funds for the launch. Nevertheless, as the first year faded to a second, I detected, in their wilting body language and covert whispers, a concern they might have to sell the property. One needs assets or income to serve longevity and even their considerable wealth will wane.

Not to mention a pressing need for a sense of purpose. They are not, like me, natural flaneurs. These men will be utterly lost if their vigilantly constructed futures evaporate, their intentions set aloft like monarch butterflies on the seasonal trek toward death. People our age need a focal point beyond work or children, or, in Fred's case, grandchildren, the progeny of one son who lives on the west coast. Rob's offspring also live far away. Sadly, he hardly knows them, he confessed, perhaps aligning himself to my childless fate.

Like all the women of my generation, I expected to bear children, but after three early miscarriages, my first husband tired of the strain, then we tired of each other. My second husband had no desire for a family, preferring full attention, and my third already had grown children who accepted me warmly, without need of mothering.

Rob's children are closer to his ex-wife and their stepfather, he being consumed most of the marriage with his professional calling and, he disclosed in an unguarded moment, one too many dalliances with nurses, and once with the wife of a critically ill patient.

Not my place to judge, I told him.

Living with aging men, I am reminded of a timeless truth: you don't get older, you get more so. At least, most of us. We do what we do and we are who we are until, or unless, we tap into the sort of person we would rather be.

None of us had hobbies beyond sport or cultural interests, denied during the pandemic, and when I suggested we learn pickleball, the new craze, on the court they installed on the inland side of the property, there was zero enthusiasm, so it sat like a prehistoric artifact, nets and equipment stored in the shed.

Thus, we meander, we swim, when we can, we read and play marathon matches of Scrabble. We tackle the daily *New York Times* crossword puzzle – Fred always finishes first. Rob and I catch up with all the documentaries we've missed, and the three of us engage often in heated political debate, trying to imagine a post-Covid era none of us could have possibly imagined.

Most mornings, I also tend the gardens, kneeling on a cushion to protect my bony knees, to feed a pageant of fledgling flowering bushes or dead-head dried blooms, such things beyond the purview of a groundskeeper who is contracted for the time being merely to mow and blow. Plants cling to their organic cycles, obliged only to their perpetuation, moderated somewhat by weather. A comfort in uncertain times. Cultivating flora is akin to cultivating young minds. I am not, however, an avid or an expert gardener. I simply follow the counsel of a former neighbor, a gifted horticulturist, to trim the unnecessary to the essential. *When in doubt, snip it out*, she advised.

A mantra for relationships as well, until I met Jack, my third husband.

Three times the charm, I believed then, but when an aneurism put a sudden end to us, I was granted occupancy of his house for a year, after which the proceeds were distributed to his sons. There wasn't much. Jack was not a man who pursued riches; he aspired instead to enlightenment. Three days a week, he advised PhD students while I tutored at the library, and often we sat together reading, or studying, after which we convened for a meal, a stroll or a film. We shared lists of places we wished to visit, and he had an incongruous Zillow fetish, so we often scrutinized homes across the globe, debating what we might do differently, or not. He would have admired the chateau, despite the excess. I miss our talks as much as the warmth of his body, his unequivocal affection, and good humor.

When his house was sold, the owner of the local bookstore, which I had frequented for thirty years, invited me to rent a tiny apartment above the shop. He suspected I was on a tight budget, and I was happy to sit at the register at busy seasons or when short-staffed. Once art was on the walls, books and knick-knacks on shelves, the sunny studio was perfectly homey. Space, I think, is an illusion, crafted by historic palaces, modern mansions, and the gurus of HGTV. We need, in truth, very little, despite my appreciation for the current habitat.

It was at the bookstore I noticed Rob. He had a full head of silvery hair and stubble along the jaw, having discarded a compulsory clean shave of the hospital life, and, unlike his brother, who has a slight paunch, he stands tall and lean. A long drink of water, as it is said. He told me later on he had noticed me at once and stopped by a few times to see me, beyond the browsing, and, the day our eyes met and held, I felt, to my surprise, a distinctive growl in the groin. My libido, I thought, had been stifled by grief. Suppressed, it turns out, not suffocated.

We chatted at first about his reading of a new translation of *War and Peace*. We shared our own war stories over coffee, a few lunches, and then, I invited him to dinner, after which he bedded me, which is a skirmish of a sort at this age. Not so much war and peace as tactical ebb and flow. From then on, it seemed we were meant to spend our final years together. We are usually on the same wave length, we like the same foods, we both require solitude, and we enjoy classical music and Irish storytellers.

I think Rob was never truly happy most of his adult life, adopting perhaps too fully the persona of stalwart savior, thus searching, as men do, for the greener grass. He says he's happy to have a good companion, and I, rapturous with Jack, and brokenhearted to lose him, I'm grateful for Rob's gentility, not to mention a new found appreciation for what a healthy body can do, at any age. Truth is, hiding out in seclusion has proven to be erotic. Skittering about stealthily like a jewel thief across the grounds, titillating, and burrowing into each other each night the reward for perseverance in strange times.

I sometimes fantasize being a courtesan. Not a concubine, a cohort. The purr of sea breezes, a foghorn in the distance, late daylight dappling across the grounds, proves seductive. Like Lady Chatterley in the forest. No wonder I find myself so often scantily clad.

The parakeet in the coal mine arrived in the form of a former colleague of Fred's, who called to ask if he might rent the inn for a long weekend. He had heard about the restoration and was in search of somewhere unique, and safe, to celebrate a momentous birthday with a large family. Fred was overjoyed. His persona bubbled up like the huge stone fountain at the entrance to the grounds, animated in a new way, and far more relatable.

And we have just enough rooms to sleep the fifteen of them, without any of us having to forego our beds, he announced excitedly.

The price he negotiated, to my mind, was outrageous, but Fred knew this customer would equate cost with value, and then, they agreed to terms. The inn would provide daily buffet breakfast and the client's own caterer imported to prepare main meals, with wine from a personal cellar, which Fred would cork without charge, having deferred the purchase.

I'll get someone in to give the pool a thorough cleaning, turn on all the fountains and spa jets, and we'll put out the stored chaises, he cried with delight, clicking the keyboard decisively as if issuing a windfall-producing equity order.

But how will they dine? I asked.

A simple question, on the surface, but which neither of the brothers, in their glee, had considered. This stopped them cold, deflated, momentarily, as they realized that, although glass-topped tables were parked in the dining room, and communal tables on the patio, chairs were never received, neither essential tabletop accoutrement like plates, glasses or silverware.

After a moment of shocked silence, the brothers made a beeline for the kitchen, and I scurried after them, watching as Fred opened one cabinet after another, as if searching for buried treasure. They both turned to me then, assuming, apparently, a woman has a magic wand to make what is missing materialize. I had to stifle my laughter – two high-powered, high-minded men brought to their knees by the simplest detail.

With a nod, I stepped up to take stock of supplies, and began to dictate a list, which Rob scrawled on a note pad, while Fred stared at me like an adolescent confounded by a study assignment. As if Mother Mary had suddenly appeared to save him. When I said I thought that would do, he grabbed the pad and rushed to his laptop to order it all, paying a colossal fee for expedited delivery. When I reminded him about chairs, he clicked again, then slammed the laptop lid with aplomb.

As if he had dispatched an astronaut to Mars.

Crisis averted, Rob said, with a wry, sexy smile, promising a special reward, later on.

And who will cook breakfast? I asked, with a different sort of smile, the smile that says, just when you thought you were in control, you're not. *Three buffet breakfasts, for fifteen guests, that's what you promised, right? Menu? Allergies and preferences? Kid food?*

The brothers were dumbfounded again.

Maybe we order in pastries and coffee urns, Rob posed.

Fred scowled. *Are you kidding? This guy is our ticket. If he's satisfied, we are on our way. Private gatherings will be in high demand as the pandemic winds down. We need first class food. Espresso and lattes, fancy teas, fresh juices. Like a French bakery.*

With this, they both turned to me again, imploringly, and again, I might have laughed. Naturally, they deferred to the woman of the house and, no matter my fierce objection to objectification, I am facile in the kitchen. These are skills that stick, like bike riding. And sex, apparently. Nonetheless, fifteen strangers who might make or break the launch of Sound Inn?

A daunting prospect.

Still, they stared at me, expectant, eyes pleading, like Dickensian orphans.

I could have said no, I should have said no, but hapless men in need are, it seems, my later life weakness, so I pointed to stools at the counter, directing them to sit, and stood before them to instruct.

Quiche, veggie and Lorraine, easy to prepare ahead of time. French Toast. We can soak overnight and bake in the morning. The smell alone will evoke a patisserie. For vegans or food fanciers, sourdough avocado toast with herbs and the option of a poached egg. Bagels and lox, de regueur. Rob, you'll cut up melons and wash berries the night before for fruit bowls. Fred, make sure to order gluten free muffins from that new age bakery in town, and arrange for espresso machines and urns for brewed coffees and teas. Also nut milks. And make sure to have yogurts and granola on hand.

I enjoyed taking charge. A rush I haven't felt since I commanded a classroom. I think we were all high on the renewal of purpose, our hearts pounding, skin flushed, soaring back to life like trees after frost, and planning to cater to our guests like the servants that once served the estate.

Fred shed his brooding self and was as gracious as a seasoned maître d'. Rob patrolled the grounds like a British butler, attending to every need. I studied the caterers to learn their technique for feeding large numbers and I flirted with a cute bartender so he might return for another gig.

The former client and his family were pleased and we breathed a sigh of relief when they left. Clean-up, however, was exhausting. Rob took on the several loads of bedding and towels, while Fred loaded the dishwashers and I scrubbed the counters and tables. I suggested it might be time to hire service staff, if we were to do this again, which seemed likely, as Fred had already updated the website to promote hygienic exclusive gatherings.

The next day, our first guests endorsed the Sound Inn on Yelp and TripAdvisor. We were on our way, so we thought, celebrating with leftover pastries and a nearly full bottle of wine left behind, until we all limped back to our rooms, sated and satisfied.

Life, and Covid, should have reminded us we never know what's coming next.

The danger of elders living on opposite ends of a large property is fear of succumbing to a life-threatening mishap, a stroke or cardiac event and the like, without a witness. Although both are hearty men, they are approaching the actuarial lifeline, and Rob was concerned we might not hear Fred if he called out for help, which is why we met for lunch most days.

If I'm missing too long, you'll come find me, Fred argued, discounting the death knell like a fluctuating bond yield.

Rob, as it turns out, was the brother to perish, when he slashed an ankle on a faulty sprinkler one morning and stumbled down to the path, bleeding far more than such a minor wound might explain. Likely blood thinners prescribed for a mild heart condition, the coroner would later pronounce. As a rule, an injury of that sort is benign, but the steady draining of blood sent him into shock, and, inexplicably, he lay without calling out as his heart gave out, despite his medical expertise.

I found him on my return from morning gardening duty and knew at once he was gone by the pallor of his skin, although I desperately pressed two fingers to his wrist, searching for a pulse, and an ear to his heart yielded nothing. I lay next to him, clinging to his hand and pressing my cheek to his.

A balmy wind blew over us, like a blessing. *Dear one*, I whispered, with a last kiss to his still warm lips.

Mortuaries were on lockdown overload and funereal gatherings discouraged, so, when Fred tried to fulfill Rob's wishes for organs to be donated, he could not. Instead, he used his negotiating prowess, and deep pockets, to arrange for an accelerated cremation and, three days later, when a plain box containing his brother's ashes was delivered, he decamped to the kitchen with his laptop and a bottle of wine, searching for a peerless vessel, and I came out of seclusion to join him.

The classiest urn for my classy little brother, he intoned, while I sat at the counter nibbling halfheartedly on a leftover pasta dish from the refrigerator, still cold, also sipping wine, until Fred ordered what he wanted, snapped his laptop shut, and then staggered to his room, thanking me as he fled, *for hanging around*.

After I cleaned up in the kitchen, back in the room I had shared with Rob, I flopped dead center on the big empty bed and wept like a girl with her first broken heart, such heartbreak the painful piercing of innocence which seems, in youth, irreparable, but inevitably heals, as such things do, until, over time, sorrows pile up and overflow like a river in heavy rains.

Again, my life in transition; an estuary, the waters of the past merging with the waters of the future, murky and slow-moving. When I contacted the bookstore owner, the flat was occupied, so I called a friend who invited me to stay with her.

We could be roommates, she suggested, having been widowed for a decade.

Elder women cohabitating in their final years makes excellent sense, but women bond. They dissect their days and their feelings. I'd rather contemplate than deliberate, so I prefer to live with a man or live alone. Nevertheless, a reprieve with a sympathetic friend seemed a good plan.

I stayed put for a week, so I would not seem to be abandoning Fred too soon, staying close, not too close, and then I packed my few belongings, and sought him out to thank him for the pleasure of my respite at the inn.

I found him perched on the west lawn like a statue, or an apparition, staring at the horizon through low lying clouds. When he turned to me, tears stained his cheeks, which incited mine, and we stood opposite in silent commiseration, sniveling and swiping at our faces like sickly kids. When I told him I was moving on, he nodded yes, without comment, although staring at me longingly, as if I might restore something to him. As if I might answer a nagging question or assuage the guilt he felt for Rob's death, as if death is negotiable.

When he stepped forward to take my hands in his, I was shaken by the warmth of his touch. The intensity of his gaze.

Bookings are coming in, he said.

I tendered an encouraging smile, and when he too smiled, I detected, for the first time, fragility in his eyes, as unpredictable as an older woman embracing her inner tramp.

How will I do this without you? he asked.

I was reminded then that men, even the most sophisticated, like Fred, are nonetheless incomplete. Missing a rib, you might say. The more accomplished, or the more emotionally mature, operate as if well put together, in spite of the gaping vacancies between the brain and the heart. Women have fewer spaces to fill and, I believe, we're innately capable of padding what may be missing with intention.

Fred stepped closer, tentatively still, his eyes beseeching.

You will hire a good chef, I said.

He nodded yes.

Maybe that cute bartender would like a job.

He smiled.

You will need to tend to all that needs tending, I said.

As you wish, he replied, and again, a nod of acquiescence. *And, when there are no guests, or, of course, whenever you feel like it, you could, you would, you are most welcome to wander...* he stammered. *Freely, if you know what I mean.*

I knew exactly what he meant.

Her Significant Other

Eliza squats on a stool watching steam rise from the bath, as if in a mystical realm. She waits, distractedly, dipping a fingertip into the water to test the temperature once, then again, until, assured she will be soothed, not singed, she disrobes, tosses her clothes into a heap, and descends, slowly, into the curved white stone, until swaddled by the warmth.

The freestanding tub is deep and long, a modernist design, like an oversized canoe, that her childhood friend, Enid, who resides in a grand house facing Lake Michigan, installed during a recent remodel to her Manhattan pied à terre. Eliza might be the first to bathe in this first class crash pad. A baptism, of a sort. She shuts her eyes, inhaling the sweet fragrance of lavender bath oil, lulled into a deeper trance, weightless and warm, beyond the stupor she's been in for days, her body, afloat, mind, adrift, her heart, nonetheless, heavy.

Eliza and Enid grew up on the same

street in Queens, a borough of New York City, just across the river from where she sits now. Bridge and tunnel girls they were called in the 70s. Children of immigrants: poor, studious, aspirational. Although their paths diverged early on, and they rarely see each other, they have stayed in touch – an occasional phone chat, holiday and birthday greetings – the bond of childhood friendship, unique. Impenetrable.

She is tall and slim, and although the tub is long, her toes grip the rim as she sinks her body to the chin to ease the tension at her neck. A former colleague, a woman convinced that every disorder or disease stems from a wounded spirit, told her grief is stored in the shoulders. Eliza suspects an aging body simply wears down.

Classical radio plays from speakers built into the walls, also assuasive. Chopin, she thinks, as she takes a deep nourishing sigh and closes her mind to refute painful thoughts. Her phone charges in the kitchen. No sense of time passing until the water goes tepid, when she sits up to turn on a thin stream of the hot to refresh, then sits back, plunging her toes into the water, knees pushed up like tree roots.

She rarely takes baths, they make her

woozy, fragile, and her own at home is shorter and shallow. In this moment, she surrenders to the calm. Grateful for her friend's generosity. On the other hand, dusk has settled in and she's alone. Best not to fall asleep in the bath.

Still, she doesn't make a move, hostage to melancholy. Shivers reverberate through her body and her stomach churns with hunger; yet, still, she soaks.

Eight hours earlier, Eliza boarded the morning Amtrak train from Providence, Rhode Island, where she fled forty years ago to make her home. She has returned today to visit with another friend of youth, the most significant of friends, Marion, her partner once in crime, low crimes of the college girl variety. Marion is surrendering to end-stage cancer and her death will be a mutual death. The final estrangement. The distance between them all these years has been tolerable. Essential. That Marion will no longer walk the city streets they once walked together, that she will no longer exist, this, for Eliza, is unfathomable.

No more the random text. The late night plaintive phone call. The intermittent missive.

Despondency chugged along the track with her this morning, like pages flipping in reverse on a calendar, from today to long ago. Dissonance to euphoria. Instead of reading, the paperback still in her bag, she stared at scenery through the smudged window. Strikingly tall trees, leaves fading on their descent to winter rest. Glimpses of the eastern bay glimmering in the morning sun. When she closed her eyes, she saw herself also in rewind, an actor in a flashback about two girls, not yet women, who merged in thrall to passion, only to be severed in favor of custom. Secrets meant to preserve tradition. Protect the innocent.

A student in a lecture she occasionally gives at the community college, a bright-eyed, serious girl studying women's history, asked her, in reference to a popular novel set in mid-20th century, *was it really like that then?*

How to explain? she pondered, in a way that seems plausible, beyond images on film, or in progressive texts, how the free love of the 60s gave way to the self-actualization of the 70s, and then, the self-indulgence of the 80s. A promising cultural evolution short circuited by conservatism. False fronts. AIDS. Censure of the other, in all its forms.

Eliza will soon say the final good-bye to the woman who brought a repressed girl to life.

The past, at last, past tense. She's not sure how she will handle this. She's already struggling with a late life identity crisis. Whatever she intended to do, she has done. Whatever she meant to be, for the most part, she has been. She sees little more in her future – what more is there beyond the shadows of the past?

She's recently retired from a satisfying career as executive editor at a small press, and freelances still with a few writers with whom she's carved out a partnership over the years. She tutors reading for migrants at the library. She has no children or grandchildren, like her ex, who packed up last year to live closer to the clan, nor family left to live near. She owns her small condo. She has a handful of good friends, the fortress against loneliness. She's recently been encouraged to write a memoir, although she sees herself as an archeologist, excavating meaning in the words. Their words, not hers.

And then, the message from Marion's husband, Ben. She knew at once why. He never makes contact, a longstanding understanding between them. In truth, he would rather Eliza had disappeared. He would message only if Marion asked him to. Her end, near.

She keeps her chin up, he texted.

Ben is famous for platitudes and Eliza was tempted to edit for detail. She knows how Marion will orchestrate her finale.

Reading the *New Yorker,* in print, she would say. Streaming crime series, fascinated by serial murderers. Listening to audio books. Savoring sweets all the more.

Eliza smiles, recalling the day Marion gobbled in two huge bites the white half of a large black and white cookie, neatly breaking off the chocolate half, not because Eliza prefers chocolate, but because Marion favored vanilla. The first time they made fudge together for Christmas gifts, and ate most of it warm from the pan. The afternoon Marion jumped for joy when they passed a bakery window display of Charlotte Russe, a 60s street pastry wrapped in a cardboard cone, and they sat on a curb licking down the Bavarian cream to sweet ladyfingers, their noses dabbed in white.

How sad it was for Eliza to watch a bold, ebullient girl who delighted in what pleases transform into a woman aiming to please. Reaching for the moon defiled by retreat, when the times demanded revolt.

Foolish to wish for more than what's been granted, Marion argued then. *Let's leave the good fight to those cut out for it,* she insisted, meaning the dedicated liberators. Hard chargers. Those willing to put themselves on the line not only for themselves.

Eliza should have visited sooner. She had no need for an invite, Ben's permission not required, whatever he believes. She used her routine as an excuse, and her penchant to stay close to home. She's something of a senescent agoraphobic these days – little beyond her immediate orbit seems significant anymore.

Significance, that's the heart of it, Marion pronounced, so many years ago, during one of their lively interminable debates.

They had both graduated college then, Marion a grant writer for the New School, Eliza a copy editor at Condé Nast.

It's not intention, not context or relevance either. Significance, that's what matters, Marion decreed, as if the conclusion to a treatise.

Defined as? Eliza asked, editorial even in conversation.

Meaning. Impact. Effect over affect.

I always thought significance has to do with worthiness, Eliza countered.

That too, yes, but beyond worth. Substance.

Yes, Eliza thought this morning on the

train. Worth. Weight. Consequence. She misses their talks, still, and the laughter. Oh, how they laughed. She was smitten from day one.

A Jew and a lass walk into a bar, Marion would say, like a standup comedian, chuckling at her cleverness.

Oversimplifying their relationship, the foreshadowing Eliza missed.

Stubborn and tenacious, the descriptors Eliza would choose. The extrovert and the loner. The traditionalist and dreamer. Pragma versus idea, Greek roots for pragmatist and idealist, she wrote in one of many manic letters to Marion she never mailed. Piles of crinkled paper, also deleted emails, marked a long path from despair.

She's in hospice care, at home, Ben texted a few days later.

Eliza's cue to come.

He did not say anything more. He kept a promise to let Eliza know, that's all. Ben was good at keeping promises, and never one to say precisely what was on his mind, certainly not to Eliza, expecting others to interpret. A man convinced early on of his significance.

At Penn Station, feeling the pressure of the clock, Eliza hailed a taxi, which stalled in chaotic traffic en route to the upper west side, where Marion and Ben have lived all these years. By the time she arrived, she was frantic, as if she might be too late. She grabbed her bags and hurried to the etched glass doors of the modest building and into a marble foyer with deco finishes. When she said Marion's name, a knowing nod from the doorman, a wave of his hand toward a musty elevator, to the top floor, to their spacious pre-war apartment with tall ceilings and windows, and dentil moldings where walls meet ceilings and floors.

Ben stood at the door like a sentinel. Eliza nearly laughed. She is no threat. Not now. In truth, not ever.

When Marion, in a phone conversation soon after Eliza fled the city, lamented his passive-aggression, Eliza accused her of taking advantage of that passivity to cement her own significance.

He's delusional if he believes you will stay with him, she argued all those years ago, shocked at Marion's decision.

Illusion, not delusion, Marion muttered.

Fine line, Eliza countered.

Litigation lawyers rely on a need to know. Only what is necessary to mount the right defense.

Ignorance being a form of bliss, Marion argued.

That's law, not life. Certainly not ethics. How can you commit to a marriage based on a lie? Why do that to him, or to me? Eliza raged.

This isn't about you, and not about us. I know what I have to do. He does not need to know more than he needs to know.

I should tell him the truth, for his sake, and for your own. How can I stand by…

Please, Eliza, Marion pleaded. *Promise me you will never betray me. He's a good man. He loves me. He has big plans for his future. Our future. He needs this as much as I do.*

She knew she could trust Eliza to stay silent. Loyal, adoring, like a puppy, she was.

She drifts in and out of consciousness, Ben explained, following a quick, perfunctory hug. *Sleeping, mostly. Not a coma. Not yet. Although, I'm not sure I will know the difference. We have a nurse now, around the clock.*

He sighed. Little changed, merely older. Forlorn. Bags under his eyes. Shadows along the jawline. Eliza felt badly for him, not the first time. She took his hand and, to her surprise, he gripped hers, tightly, in need of comfort, even from her, before he pulled away, the source of the comfort flawed.

Eliza, his nemesis. The keeper of secrets.

The apartment was unchanged. Ben and Marion share a predilection for constancy. The same oversized mahogany and oak furnishings gifted to them from an aged aunt when they married. Turkish area rugs, faded where the afternoon sun streams in, despite heavy drapes lining the windows.

A stifling, acrid aroma of ammonia and rubbing alcohol swept over her. The scent of sterility. The scent of sickness. As if she had stepped into a mortuary, or a wake, and she has a sudden instinct to flee, although she will not. Not yet.

Ben parked her travel bag and purse in the kitchen. He handed her a glass of water, which she gulped down thirstily, and waited, like a servant, no small talk, before leading her down the hall to their bedroom. As they passed the guest room, Eliza noticed an open sofa bed with rumpled sheets. The nurse, she assumed, although these old apartments have a cramped maid's room in back. Ben, more likely, forced, or choosing to sleep alone, sooner than later.

As they approached the room, a nurse, a mannequin in silhouette, stood at attention. Another sentinel.

No change, she reported to Ben, who suggested she take a break.

She nodded to him, and to Eliza, who murmured her thanks as she passed.

One thing she was certain of: Ben would guarantee the best care for Marion. She lived, and will die, peacefully, if not at peace.

Eliza sat on the dining chair positioned at the pillow where Marion rested her head. Daylight glinted around the window shades, the light refracted, as if in a holy place. She might have shared a laugh with Marion at this – they were both fiercely agnostic – and she wondered suddenly what burial arrangements have been made.

She shook her head free of gloom. Time enough for logistics.

Ben lingered at the door. *I'll just make a fresh pot of tea, and we have some sandwiches, from the deli down the street, if you like,* he said.

She looked up to him. *Rest a bit, Ben. You must be knackered. I'll keep her company.*

He paused, relenting or reluctant, she could not be sure, before turning away.

Many years into the marriage, the secret was revealed. Marion called in tears. Ben was aghast, she told Eliza. *Blinded by love.*

How long have you been with her? Eliza asked, certain that only a serious relationship would prompt discovery.

Too long to dismiss easily, Marion replied.

Eliza, having been so easily dismissed, for the first time felt sorry for Ben.

I will not humiliate him, Marion said.

This seems a good time to live an honest life, Eliza said. *Wouldn't Ben rather a true marriage?*

Until death do us part, Marion retorted. Resigned. Resolute.

Seated at Marion's bedside, watching her rest on her way to death, Eliza revisits all of it again, and she wonders now if there is anything she might say or do to help Ben reconcile the choice he made to stay the course. Perhaps he has, more than she. Then again, understanding is not the same as forgiveness. Forgiveness is not forgetting.

Marion lay flat on her side of a king-size bed, the subtle rise and fall of her chest the only realization of life. Her body, smoothed under a lightweight quilt, a mere replica of the woman she was. Eliza took her hand, cool to the touch, not cold, as flimsy as the wing of a bird. Hardly the fiery collegiate who offered her hand to Eliza at freshman weekend so long ago.

The branches of New York City's public university were free then to city students and populated by eastern European descendants, like Marion, and Irish, like Eliza, who could not have afforded private higher education. No dormitories or football stadiums, no sweeping campuses, rather imposing Gothic buildings dotting modest plots of land in each of the five boroughs of the city, patches of grass along paved pathways, and student centers crowded with ambition and hope. Commuter students, living with their parents, they crammed the morning classes in order to work afternoons or nights to pay for textbooks, a diner dinner or a Saturday night out, then home to study, sleep hard and fast until dawn, energized by self-discovery and possibilities.

Eliza, shy, anxious, sat that first day on her sweater, shaded by a still full canopy of an oak tree, immersed in a book. What was she reading? Brontë, perhaps. Or Woolf. Writers on the recommended reading list who would revolutionize her outlook and chart her career. Marion, trotting by on her way to a mandatory gathering, stopped short when she noticed her there and glared, as if Eliza were committing an atrocity in public. She leaned down to grab the book from her hands and glanced at the title, nodding approvingly, before marking the page with a fold and snapping it shut.

Eliza, bewildered more than bothered, took the measure of the meddler. She wore bell bottom jeans, hems straggling on the ground. A black T-shirt, inscribed with the school logo, hugged ample breasts, and a peace pendant dangled between. She had long, sandy hair. Exceedingly large, jade green eyes. Lean arms tanned and muscular from a summer job tending campers at a Brooklyn beach.

A sophomore at the college, Marion had been tapped to initiate the uninitiated, as she would do, again and again, for Eliza.

Plenty of time ahead for reading, get up and come with me, Marion pronounced, reaching out a hand to pull Eliza to standing.

With that gesture, Eliza came to life, like a sapling, withered in the heat, roused by rains. Throughout her college years, to their tentative first steps into adulthood, Marion would pull Eliza up, one way or another, until she brutally let her down.

Eliza studied her face now as she slept, the beauty of the girl forfeited to age, marred by disease. Her nose sloped, facial skin slack and pale, nearly gray, like her hair, flattened to her head. Her affect, also flat. This alone would mark the death knell.

A sob rose into Eliza's throat, which she swallowed down. She took a few deep breaths to settle her heartbeat and speak.

I took the train down, she said, her voice shattering the solemnity in the room. *I tried to decipher the code,* she said, more softly, alluding to a game they once played to pass the time on long subway rides, inventing personal lives for passengers based on clothes or shoes, even knowing, so well, the cover shields the story.

This young man, no more than thirty, sat opposite, wearing stylish jeans, perfectly pressed, and a vest over a starched blue shirt, buttoned, no tie, and black canvas sneakers with thick, spotlessly white soles, Eliza described, as if they were just having coffee. *It's all about sneakers these days, right? A fledgling music producer, maybe? A young architect trying to look cool for an interview? I suspect his girlfriend, maybe boyfriend, helped him stage the look. Could be anyone. I've lost my touch. The game has gone the way of the charlotte russe.*

She half expected Marion to bolt up and challenge her point of view when she noticed her eyes rippling under the lids. Perhaps she heard Eliza's voice. Perhaps she knew she was by her side. More likely dreaming, Eliza knew, but what dreams might she have, having given up on her dreams so long ago?

Eliza shifted in her chair to stretch her stiffening spine, then went on to describe the bright blue sky on the trip this morning. The first ochre and red leaves. Then she described a volunteer gig she had taken on recently, how weary she was after three hours shepherding guests at a fundraising luncheon.

The proceeds go to a women's shelter, but after being at attention, you know, guiding guests to auction tables and such, for so long, my legs were screaming for relief. I got roped in by a friend. I wanted to be useful. Help raise money for the needy.

People need the needy, the needy give us meaning, Marion once said, as if alluding to Eliza, who cringed now at that recollection.

Marion's lips curled at the corners, and like a skeleton in a horror movie, she opened her eyes, staring straight ahead, before turning toward Eliza, who cried out with joy.

Hello you!

Marion's eyes were vacant. Bloodshot. Pupils dilated. No sign of recognition, only the enervation of pain, the breakdown of the body.

Perhaps the effect of palliative medication. Or was it a lifetime of denial?

That first year they were together, and the years that followed, it was Marion who introduced Eliza to herself. She the one to help her find her groove, Marion liked to say. Eliza's body sprung to life at her touch. Her tutelage. She finally understood why she felt so little at the urgent groping of adolescent boys or the closet kissing games that left her cold. The men on the subway pushing their boners to her butt or the lecherous calls from others on the street on a winter day: *I'll make you warm, baby.*

The different desire she could not name.

What is wrong with me? she cried into her pillow at night, ashamed to speak of it and no one to ask, until Marion.

Her savior. Her first love. To Eliza's mind, still, her one true love.

They began with overnights in the apartments of compassionate friends, quietly indulging their fevered urgings and, for Eliza, tutelage. After Marion graduated, they shared a studio apartment, splitting expenses the perfect pretense. At night, they clung to each other for fortitude, as well as pleasure. After hours, they sipped beer at a bar with no name, or a bistro they referred to as *the pub*: wood-paneled, smokey and cheap, blending in with a mix of graduate students and the so-called young upwardly mobile.

Ben arrived one night as a new bartender. Swarthy and stocky, like a sailor, he was amiable. Well educated. He watched over female patrons, being the sort of man wanting to make a woman feel safe. He turned out to be a third year law student at NYU.

What a surprise, Marion said. *A bartender with a brain.*

Total bore, Eliza pronounced, sensing at once, inexplicably, a threat.

He invited Marion to dinner.

Imagine, an actual date! she cried. *I mean, pizza, I'm sure, but so what?*

Why go out with him? Eliza asked.

Why not? Marion answered.

I should think the answer to that is obvious, Eliza snapped.

What is between us is between us. Out in the world, that's another thing, Marion replied.

Are you kidding? We're the reformation, Eliza countered.

We are an affront to motherhood and apple pie, Marion argued. *An offense to Judeo-Christian values, sex meant to procreate. Period.*

Eliza was stunned by her rhetoric. *Where is this coming from?*

Options. It's about options, Eliza.

We're feminists!

Feminism is about equal rights and equal pay. And orgasms. Marion laughed. *Women like us, we're not part of the protest, yet.*

Eliza, however, could not imagine a life without Marion, even if closeted. Like Virginia Woolf and Vita Sackville-West. Poet Elizabeth Bishop and her Brazilian architect. Hushed voices. Secreted pleasures. Until the culture evolved, which she was certain it would.

She lost Marion to Ben on Sunday nights and then, more frequently. She slept too often alone. She tried to be sympathetic, although affronted by Marion's yearning to blend in. To appear, as she defined, normal. Weeks turned into months as Eliza clung to the belief Marion would soon come to her senses, and each time Marion returned, she begged forgiveness, but without remorse or reassurance.

Eliza waited her out.

The night it all fell apart, Marion was at the apartment waiting for Eliza to return after a night out with colleagues.

We've set a date, she announced, flashing a tiny glittering engagement ring.

Oh my god, you're not serious? Eliza cried. *What are you thinking? This is not who you are.*

Who I am? I am me. I want children. I want the life our mothers want us to have. All of it.

Eliza was struck dumb.

We were girls, sweetheart, Marion cajoled. *Curious girls. Sightseeing. Sowing oats.*

Five years sowing oats? Eliza whimpered.

Marion seemed for a moment to relent. Tears sprang to her eyes. She slid closer to Eliza on the couch, so close Eliza melted into her embrace, like a wounded child.

We are more, Marion whispered. *We are love. We shall always be. But I have to be what my grandparents hoped for. What our parents have made possible for us. I cannot disappoint them.*

Eliza pulled away. *So you will fuck a man the rest of your life?*

Marion recoiled. *I will find what pleasure I can find and reap the rewards.*

You will commit to a fake marriage? Deceive a decent man?

Marion swiped defiantly at her tears.

Eliza, please. We do the best we can do. My parents are innocents. My sister and brothers are coming up. I'm first, I set the tone. They adore Ben. I will not ruin their dreams.

Their dreams are more important than your own? More important than who you are?

Their dreams are more important than yours! And my dream is to live up to theirs. That's what we do for the people we love.

There it was. Marion did not love Eliza sufficiently to consider her dream their dream. She was not significant after all.

Within weeks, Eliza applied to graduate school and left the city soon after. She refused to attend Marion's wedding. She took two jobs to save for a master's degree and worked evenings and weekends until completed. She found pleasure in promiscuity. She discovered the shelter of wine. A woman with whom she thought she might make a life lasted just long enough to heal a small part of her broken heart, and incite the courage to seek another.

What irony it was when, within a few years, Marion discovered she was infertile, and Ben refused to adopt.

He's seen how damaged abandoned children are, even babies. We're not up to that task, Marion told Eliza, when she called seeking comfort.

How selfish can he be? Eliza argued. *And*

you, Marion. If you're going to live a lie, why not compensate by saving a lost child.

I'm not sure I have what it takes, Ben's right about that.

So, leave him now. End the charade. You no longer have a reason to stay, Eliza pleaded.

I made a vow. Reason enough.

By then, Eliza was completing studies at Brown University and working at a fledgling literary press, where she would rise over time to executive editor.

Marion and Ben lived satisfying lives, on the surface. She surely had lovers, but she never revealed, not to Ben, nor Eliza, who found love, for a time, and then again, for a long time. None, forever. None, Marion.

You were, you are, my one true love, Eliza whispered to her silent diminished friend.

At that, Marion turned toward Eliza, her eyes closed, but her arm outstretched like a tree limb torn in the wind. Eliza gripped her hand, wishing she could raise her from the dead as Marion long ago raised her with the grasp of a hand from loneliness and confusion.

What might she be saying with that gesture? Eliza wondered. Forgive me? Stay with me? No way to know and no matter now.

Marion's breathing deepened, slower yet steady. After a few moments, Eliza pressed her cheek to hers, before tenderly kissing her lips, which were distressingly cool. She let go of Marion's hand and fled the room.

Ben sat at the kitchen table, before him a half cup of tea, likely tepid, and remnants of a sandwich, its edges bitten to a rocky creek bed.

Eliza slumped into the chair opposite.

Hard to see her this way, isn't it?

Eliza nodded. She thought she should say something, words of comfort for Marion's husband, but nothing came to mind.

I think I'll settle into my friend's apartment for the night and I'll be back in the morning, if that's all right, she said.

Of course, Ben answered, rising from his chair to escort her to the door.

She made her way in reverse from the apartment to the elevator to the street, the late-day air, even if saturated with the scent of city detritus, refreshing, filled with life, and then, to ground herself in the city, reclaim the girl she was, she boarded a crosstown bus and watched the cityscape pass, the neon lights, the bustle, the panorama of people, slowly walking six blocks, peeking into ground-level brownstone windows, imagining the perfect lives within, as she used to do when she was a girl.

At the apartment, she dropped her bag in the hall, plugged her phone to charge in the kitchen, and wandered from room to room, admiring the sophisticated furnishings and fine art, and the expansive view, and then, she filled the bath.

She has no idea how long she's been soaking. Her skin is soggy. She's shivering. She wrenches herself to stand, steps out and grabs an oversized bath towel to dry, then reaches for the plush white terry robe hanging behind the door, pulling the belt tight to her waist and the collar to her neck, the soft fabric a comfort.

In the kitchen, she glances at her phone. Ben has called and left a voice message.

Marion has passed.

She slumps into a chair as the words sink in. She had assumed, when this moment came, she would collapse with grief. Weep as piercingly and uncontrollably as she had for months after they separated. Instead, she feels no greater sorrow than at the end of a sad story, lamenting what cannot be revised or restored. And, oddly, she's glad now she did not say good-bye. She will mourn her beloved friend in the memory of youthful joy. The memory of first love.

When she calls, Ben answers at once, and after the obligatory words expressing her sympathy, she tells him, *you were a wonderful husband, Ben.*

Thanks, thank you, he stammers, her praise unexpected. *I'm glad you were here, Eliza. I have more calls to make. Plans to make. Tomorrow, noonish, come back to the apartment. Her brothers and sister will be here. I'll confirm the time. And, and I'll let you know the schedule…* he pauses. *For the interment, I mean. Very soon.*

I'm not sure I will stay in town, Eliza replies, wanting no part of communal grief, nor further perpetuation of pretense.

Well, I'll let you know, so you'll know. And, thanks again for coming.

Eliza imagines his relief, her presence a reminder of what he would rather forget.

She waits for the tears that do not come. Perhaps she has grieved long enough.

Her stomach growls. Her head aches. In the refrigerator she discovers two prepackaged salads and a baguette wrapped in foil. White wine, chilled. Red wine in a counter rack. Enid, a thoughtful hostess. The friend she can count on. She will have to tell her about Marion, thank her for the solace of this space, but not now. She could not bear sympathies, not yet.

She puts the baguette into the oven to warm, uncorks and pours a glass of red wine, and plates a salad, drizzling olive oil and red vinegar over the top to toss. She retrieves and slices the baguette, watching as the butter she slathers over it melts, until barely visible. When she sits at the small round table nestled to the kitchen window, she raises her glass to Marion, dearly departed, and drinks, before she eats enough to appease the hunger.

Street lamps below illuminate the city, and as she sips another glass of wine, she leans closer to the window to watch the scene below: cars, buses, taxis, and a throng of pedestrians, waiting at street corners, rushing through cross walks, on their way home to family or meeting friends for dinner. Perhaps, searching for love.

A shiny new epicurean coffee machine on the counter catches her eye. As tired as she is, she cannot imagine she will sleep tonight, so she brews espresso, the scent alone nourishing. She sits pensively as it cools some and then she sips, rolling the rich brew over her tongue as she was taught, long ago, at an east village panetteria, where she often sat with Marion at a dusty, wobbly, metal bistro table set on the sidewalk, chatting about the day, waving their hands in the air dramatically, while faking an Italian accent between bites of biscotti. She can taste even now the tart almond, pistachio, anise flavors cutting the sweetness. She can almost feel the crumbs on her lips. She can see the delight in Marion's bright, beautiful smile, as they savored each mouthful, savoring each other, pretending to be the women they would have liked to be.

Transcendence

When Bill returned home, late in the day, after another demanding workday, he found his wife, Loretta, in the living room, nose to nose in conversation with a stranger, and rather than interrupt or interrogate the scene, he stood in the foyer to observe.

A few sprigs of daylight streamed into the room through French doors facing the back patio, lighting the pair, as if on stage. Loretta wore her daily costume: black leggings with a black turtleneck, the sleeves rolled into cuffs revealing firm flexors, but not toned in a gym, rather a lifetime playing violin. With shaggy silvery hair grazing her neck and a pixie-like build, she is frequently mistaken for a dancer, similarly precise in stance – shoulders squared, spine stick straight – body language as integral to her vocation as the bow.

An odd couple they were, Bill thought, his lithe, diminutive wife and a burly stranger wearing faded jeans, a plaid shirt and a quilted vest, his cheeks shadowed by late day stubble. The slump to his shoulders hinted he might have rushed to this meeting after his own long workday and Bill recognized him at once as the sort of working man subject to freak accidents he often tends to at the hospital. A roofer, or a painter, although, didn't they paint inside and out a few years back, and shingled the roof? Or maybe longer. Time blurs with age.

A full head shorter, Loretta looked up to him as she spoke, although she stood so solidly on her feet, face ignited with certainty, she might have been the expert, and he the acolyte. He listened, attentively, cocking his head now and then, scanning images or entering notes with an index finger onto a tablet he held in the other hand, his gaze otherwise following the long finger she pointed to the patio, across the room toward the street, and then to the ceiling.

Bill wondered now if the roof sprung a leak, the source of the leak difficult to identify as water rarely travels in a straight line on its quest to ground level, confounding even the best roofers. Like Loretta, he thought, with a smile, water flowing as she sways to the music, her body curved to the violin.

On the other hand, he's certain she

would have mentioned a leak, and he has seen no signs of seepage. Something else was amiss, and for some reason, Bill will never be certain why, he had a powerful sensation of doom.

Zoning, the man remarked, and Loretta nodded. *Permits*, he added. She nodded again. *Engineering*, he said, emphatically, and she responded, with equal conviction, *understood*.

Bill sighed. His wife is on a mission, for sure, but he will have to wait for her to reveal what she has in mind. She responds poorly if pressured, worse when obstructed.

It was that certitude that drew Bill to Loretta from the first, in contrast to her graceful persona on stage. She is not a woman to be underestimated. Whatever she has in mind, she deliberates with the same scrupulous attention to notation on a music score.

Bill's curiosity, and apprehension, now piqued, stepped forward into the room for an introduction.

We have much to discuss, Loretta said, to Bill and, parenthetically, to what turned out to be a contractor, as they shook hands.

I have my homework, I'll get back, pronto, he said, shaking Loretta's hand before slipping away, leaving little trace he'd been there at all.

Smart man, Bill thought. Like a priest or a bartender, the less said, the better.

Loretta thrives on what Bill would call controlled variation, like the movements of a sonata. His days, in contrast, as chief of staff for a hospital emergency center, are defined by persistent sharp turns in direction. He adapts as quickly as a chameleon changes color at the first sign of peril. Once at home, he requires a sustained current of consistency. Despite their different temperaments, their relationship has lasted forty years, an achievement they take pride in. They've had their share of disputes, as all marriages do, and have survived a few near-fatal collisions, and, at moments like these, he's reminded of her grace, and sharp mind, also her grit, to which he is alternately target or ally.

What he saw in her smile, however, was unsettling: smug satisfaction.

An addition? Bill cried, flabbergasted, when Loretta declared what she had in mind. *What for? We never wanted more space even when the kids were home, why now?*

Let's have a glass of wine, she replied, in a tone of voice a school teacher might deploy to cajole a frustrated child, taking his hand to lead him toward the kitchen where, Bill suspected, he was headed into an ambush. Not the first, although he long ago accepted his role in their partnership, to which he is well suited. More than a partner, Bill is her nest: a warm, trusted place, sheltered from the elements, and from which she can soar to her desired heights at will, before settling back. In return, she is his north star, beckoning him to safe harbor from the choppy seas of his days.

The moment he entered the kitchen, an aroma of soup simmering on the stove calmed his nerves, the mélange of onion, potato and squash, perfect comfort food. Likely planned. His pulse rate slowed. He took a breath and sat, starving as well as fatigued, having been bombarded all day by patients in need, and stymied by short staffing.

When their son and daughter were children, rambunctious and rowdy, there was an understanding that when Bill returned from the hospital, the decibel level must come down. Home, their designated sanctuary. Where their teenage children brought schoolmates to feast on baguettes and cheeses Loretta purchased at a French market twice a week to entice them from the dangers beyond. Where she stages cozy dinners with close friends, where the strains of her violin resound throughout the house, and where she often hums to a tune only she can hear, stirred by bird songs or a melody on the wind.

The place where they will return from extended travels, he hopes, when he retires next year, a plan for which they've worked and saved, and which is, at last, within reach.

What Loretta had in mind was therefore particularly jarring.

She grabbed a bottle of red wine already open on the counter, and two glasses from the cabinet, setting them on the breakfast table where they share meals since the kids moved on, the dining table reserved for guests.

Loretta sat adjacent, instead of opposite, pulled her chair closer to the table, and to Bill, smiling as she poured the wine.

We can turn the living room into a dedicated music space. A conservatoire, you might say, she nearly whispered, as if, by quiet explication, she might not be debated.

The same way she coaxes notes from her violin, or soothed the children when they wept; a tone of voice as comforting as conclusive, although, in this moment, not one that makes a man feel like he has a say in the matter.

Bill took a sip of the wine, pretending to process what was, to his mind, absurd. Loretta may be a change agent, but she's rarely foolish, nor outrageous. Why would she envision a conservatory in the home where their children grew up. They've paid it off now; all theirs, they celebrated, the day of the final mortgage payment. A simple home, a traditional colonial in walking distance to the center of an agrestic southern Connecticut town populated with 19th century architecture. White siding, federal blue shutters, and a black front door, open to a foyer dividing a square dining room from a rectangular living room, a fireplace at its center. Double doors at back lead to a large patio. A baby grand piano fills the bay window facing front. A country-style kitchen leads to a family room in the truest sense – the reading and media viewing room, board game-playing room, and, until a few years ago, workspace at a desk built into one wall of bookshelves. Upstairs, three bedrooms – the two formerly occupied by children now a guest room and a designated home office.

They need no more than this, their home as integral to their lives as each other, and all Bill has required or wanted, and, he believed,

Loretta as well, until now.

There was a brief pause between them, Loretta sipping the wine while Bill took time to assess, as a good physician will do. She ran one finger down the stem of her glass, strumming, in effect, a tick she's acquired in recent years, as if, without a violin, she feels incomplete.

The string-stringer, Loretta calls herself, having struck long ago the challenging wife-mother-career balance by becoming a contract player rather than a member of a symphony or chamber group. She substitutes with touring companies short a violinist or fills a chair with local orchestras vacated by illness or personal leave. Her manager handles her bookings, also grievances, which are frequent, because when it comes to music, Loretta is as tightly strung as her strings. She has a history of conflict with a conductor or lead musician, not one to silence herself, and often justified, her music instincts impeccable, although a compulsion to correct, insufferable.

Gone frequently during evening hours, sometimes on tour weeks at a time, Bill and the children flowed through their days more like a jazz trio than an orchestra, and when Loretta returned, buoyed like a creek bed replenished by winter rains, they all glided seamlessly back to her syncopation, until the next movement.

The word conservatoire from the Latin root, conservare, means to preserve, Loretta explained, breaking the strained silence. *Or, conservatorio, in Italian, also a hospital for foundlings, that's what it was, did you know that? Of course you did. A charming word for an awful thing, leaving a baby in a cold dark doorway.* She shook her head sadly. *Music is the womb. Source and sustenance. These days, we've lost the previous intimacy. The bonding of musicians and audience. So, what I have in mind is an expanded family room to serve as a living room. We already live there, right? With a new bedroom above, for us…*

Why a new master? he inquired, seeking a modicum of clarity in his confusion.

They call it a primary bedroom now, she quipped. *To elevate the ceiling in the living room, to install state of the art acoustics.*

As Bill began to speak, Loretta raised a palm to deflect protest, and stood. *Shall I serve the soup? The bread is warm.*

Loretta, sit down, please. Dinner can wait. What's going on? These are major decisions you're making. Costly decisions. Life-altering. What is this really about?

Just brainstorming, Bill. This contractor has a superb reputation. The one who did Sharon and Lou's renovation. You were impressed, remember? Let's see what he does with the plans.

You're going right to plans?

We need engineering, visuals, to determine what's feasible. Permits. Estimates. And I have time now, I turned down the gig.

You turned down the chance to work with the Israeli? What's his name?

Lahav Shani.

You said he's the one young conductor you most wanted to work with.

Maybe too young. And with what's going on there…

He's too young? Bill echoed, having never heard her say this before.

He's still in his thirties! Lord.

So? You said he's the real deal.

Yes, but not sure we would get on. Besides, would have been a short run. Very intense. I want to be home to keep up the heat. Long way to go before we sort this out.

Bill, flummoxed, growing angrier by the second, took a deep breath to steady himself, and then another, before he spoke.

Loretta, let's be practical. The town will not

permit this anyway. A music hall in a residential neighborhood? They've restricted vacation rentals, they won't give this a green light. Why go to the trouble, and considerable expense, to face refusal?

Loretta nodded, placing a hand gently on his arm, to neutralize the opposition.

Where there's a will, there's a way.

He stared at his wife a few seconds, then took a slug of wine for ballast.

Bill's first instinct always is triage: stem the bleeding, assess the damage, determine the best treatment. However, he was not ready yet to probe the core question, not after the day he's had. He will soon have to ask: what's missing? Has she been yearning for a dramatic change, not so much a midlife but a late life crisis? Is there a threat of which he's unaware? The greater dilemma will be how to help her get what she needs without toppling their equilibrium or precluding plans for the last phase of their lives.

As if reading his mind, Loretta said, *sweetheart, a new adventure, that's all. From home! The way of the millennium, right? Remote work, remote music, so to speak. Bear with me. Let's follow the bread crumbs to see what's possible.*

Before he could speak, she smiled and

said, *I know I can count on you.*

He nodded. Of course. She relies on his unequivocal support. She always has. Bill is the one person on earth who gets her, Loretta says. He takes great pride at being a reliable partner. Adaptable and understanding. They've settled into their empty nest well, they agree, beyond the profound sensation of loss when a family is no longer intact. What he compares to the ache of a phantom limb and what Loretta describes as a minor chord, which sounds, at first, dissonant, or morose, but which underscores tension, she says, and amplifies the pleasure of the ensuing harmony.

The pandemic lockdown was especially difficult for her. Bill took on longer hours at the hospital, while she spent all day and often into the night at home, alone. Their children were living and working on their own by then, and at Bill's urging, stayed in place. Loretta was delighted at first, she claimed, to play hours on end, uninterrupted, what she's not been able to do since she was a student, or early in her career, before children were born. She looked forward to alternating technique. Exploring interpretation. To her surprise, the isolation proved soul crushing. For months, she drifted through the house as if displaced, kidnapped and held hostage indoors. After a few months, in defense, she decided to play for neighbors. Fridays, at dusk, she set her music stand and chair on the driveway, while the locals spread out on blankets and folding chairs, children frolicking happily, sometimes hushed by the magic of music. Loretta played mostly elegies by Shostakovich or Stravinsky – melancholic, mournful evocations of loneliness and broken hearts, broken spirits – always adding a short uplifting piece as the finale.

Bill wonders now if prolonged solitude, the anxiety of persistent jeopardy, germinated into the madness of a home-based music space.

Loretta, maybe we need to explore new ways of living, he submitted, as she refilled his wine, then ladled and presented steaming, fragrant bowls of soup. *The upside of retirement, right? The post-Covid world is shapeshifting, yes, and I know how much chamber music means to you, but to suddenly dip so deep into our savings for a questionable construction project? To become an impresario? This is an extreme response.*

He sipped the first spoonful of soup, its warmth seeping into him, bolstering his mood. *Good,* he murmured.

Loretta cooks simple hearty meals and Bill is always appreciative.

Bill, I've been lying awake nights thinking about this for some time, while you, of course, sleep like a baby.

She smiled, endearingly, but then, her expression turned somber.

I've been increasingly frustrated with the business of music, you know that. All that matters is the halls be filled. Sponsors flattered ad nauseum. A new generation of stars cultivated and marketed with toned bodies and stage antics, like gymnasts at the Olympics. I am sick of the hype. The artificiality of it, no matter how good the music, no matter how good the players. This is not what classical music ought to be.

It's not what anything should be, although the business of music has always been so, Bill said. *The piper must be paid. Same for medicine. We've gone from care to custodian, remediation to quick fix. This is the nature of the modern age.*

If you were in charge, medicine would be truly progressive, and caring. Do no harm.

And that's just it. I am not in charge. Nor you. We make peace with what we can do.

Yes, but many of us want to make music merely for the sake of the music. Return to our roots.

Play for music lovers, not status seekers. We're still in our sixties. I have no desire to slow down. Golf and gardening, not for me, or you. We will travel, definitely. Plenty of time for that, barring another deadly virus or economic disaster. I want to play a lot longer. I want to make a difference.

There was a poignancy in her voice he had not heard in some time and he recognized the necessity for empathy for what was yet to be revealed. No further protest, not now. Loretta will make her case over time, and steadily, like a metronome.

More to the point, Bill was confident the city's planners, the neighbors, maybe the music community, would shut her down.

That night, in bed, where they share the most intimate feelings, Loretta snuggled to Bill, broader than she, taller than she, so that she curls into his body like a treble clef. Fresh from a shower, seductively fragrant lavender cream saturated her skin, and coconut oil sparkled on her fingers, a balm against the dryness of chalk.

Do you remember when I told you about my final exam at Oberlin? So long ago, you may not recall, and I'm not sure I told you everything.

Tell me again, he said, charmed by her fragrance, her warm body.

These the moments that make all moments possible.

Students can petition to be exempt from a jury examination with a recital, and strings were permitted to play in ensemble. Jenny, on viola, you remember her. Carl on cello. The second violin, a girl I lost touch with, I think she still teaches, in Boston. We played Haydn, of course.

Of course?

Loretta tsked. *You must know this by now.*

Remind me.

The father of the string quartet! Although you know I prefer Beethoven.

I do know that.

She pressed a hand to his heart, which he covered with his. The sign, since they were married, they are one.

The performance was crucial to our final standing. I was top tier through school, but never at the top. None of us were. We matched up well. And I was at my best that day. She sighed, wistfully. *The constant critique, for me, as you might imagine, was impatience. I was, I am, still, too often an eighth note ahead. Hard to match the meter sometimes.*

Under cover of darkness, Bill smiled. As he might describe his entire life with Loretta.

That day, we were starlings in flight. A

murmuration. And even in the midst of that perfect alignment, I had the revelation, which I'd suspected for some time, I would never be better than my best that day.

Loretta...

She put a finger to his lips. *I don't need a pep talk, Bill. There's no bandage for what I feel. Exceptionalism is exceptional. The rest, at best, satisfactory. I listen, I play, I swell to music I love, and I persist, because the persistent survive. I'm a working musician and that's no small feat. I knew then I will never be better than I am. Talent is a continuum. I fall among the best of the middling. What I can do, what I think I'm meant to do, now, is make a home for the rest of us. Play for people who may not be as sophisticated, or as self-conscious, as the crowds at symphony halls, not to mention those who can no longer afford a ticket. A cozy setting for chamber music lovers, played by the best of the rest.*

She shifted her body closer to Bill and leaned up to press her lips to his, the sort of kiss that says, don't fail me now. Bill will not, of course, because he always hopes for the best, while prepared for the worst. The paradigm of emergency medicine.

And then, she strummed his chest like a violin – the signal of her desire.

As they slept that night, she reached for his hand, as she always has, after they make love, holding on through the night. Their union as potent at rest as at dawn. Bill, however, lay awake, pondering how he might provide the support his wife needs without compromising their plans for the years ahead, the years no longer captive to work or obligated to family, rather to reaping the reward of lives well lived.

He wondered, for the first time, if they were no longer on the same page, and at a dinner later in the week, the conversation shed further light on the page Loretta had turned.

They were at the home of neighbors, small business proprietors who have lived in this area thirty years, and equally immune to the prevailing propaganda that bigger, bolder, or newer, means better. The other couple at the table: younger neighbors, high school teachers, who share their sentiments.

They have extraordinary dexterity and the passion of youth, the music teacher commented on the new generation of classical musicians.

What do you think, Loretta? Are they that good? his wife, a history teacher, asked.

Some, absolutely, she answered. *Excellent technicians. Stylists. Overflowing with charisma.*

That's for sure. Who would you single out? the music teacher inquired.

The Australian, Christian Li. Youngest ever winner of the Menuhin competition. A sensation on the stage. Interesting selections. And Johan Dalene, the Swede. Superb melodic expression.

Indeed. And Maria Duenas? Quite the star.

Ah, the Spaniard. Looks like a tango dancer. Incredible G-string. Big on baroque, and Lalo.

Big on Facebook, he remarked.

They know how to use social media, for sure, the host chimed in.

I wouldn't know, Loretta retorted.

Don't forget the young German, Jonian Ilias Kadesha, the music teacher said. *A virtuoso.*

Loretta nodded. *Did you know, as if insult to injury, these progenies are loaned violins crafted centuries ago? Duenas plucks a Nicolo Gagliano!*

Maybe the strings retain their DNA, Bill proposed. *Every fingertip leaves an imprint.*

Babies with bows, Loretta muttered.

They do seem younger than ever, Bill said.

Everyone is younger than ever, the hostess said, and they all laughed, resigned.

The other day, a video of a young Russian violinist came into my Instagram feed, the music teacher said. *Playing on a city street, Mozart, but with a beat, like a pop song. Springy ponytail and a short floppy skirt. Sidewalk tip jar, of course.*

Hard to distinguish a true classicist from a talented troubadour, his wife commented.

On the other hand, young'uns seem to be making symphonic music mainstream, he said.

Are they? Bill asked.

I read the other day that theater audiences have not returned to pre-Covid levels, and dance is struggling, but classical music has roared back. Larger and younger audiences.

Not sure you can connect the dots to this new breed, Loretta said. *Shakespeare keeps finding new audiences as well.*

True. One hopes a new generation will save all the classics from extinction. I would think you would be pleased, he argued.

Loretta was not at all pleased. She has been haunted by images of perky girls dancing with their violins on the sidewalk like fiddlers, a term she despises. Nearly as off-putting as young first violinists on stage wearing stiletto heels and body hugging dresses slit to the hip, as if strutting an awards show red carpet.

In the days following the dinner, Loretta listened over and over to an album of Duenas playing Beethoven and then she studied videos of her playing Paganini, who, according to popular legend, made a Faustian pact with Satan granting him magical powers to seduce sound and vibrato beyond the reach of mortal violinists. What was called the devil's music.

Loretta began to picture all the young charismatic musicians as devilish, and she, an avenging angel.

The concert hall is a modern phenomenon, not the only way, she lamented one night, as she plopped onto a chair opposite Bill in the family room and picked up a new issue of the *New Yorker,* flipping its glossy pages perfunctorily before tossing it aside.

Bill looked up from reading a mystery by an Irish writer he admires. Playing softly in the background, Miles Davis, his maestro.

You're not planning to take to the streets are you? he blurted, meaning to lighten the mood and regretting the comment the moment his words were uttered.

Of course not, she snapped. *Really, Bill!*

Honey, you used to say the halls brought serious music to a broader audience, he cajoled.

Maybe that's the problem, she grumbled. *Classical music is not mass market. Not passive, like streaming. It's like reading a good book,* she said, gesturing to his. *Engaging. Feeds the imagination. Chamber music should be played in a chamber, not an amphitheater. Classical music will go the way of classic literature. Art films. Nothing but bestsellers and blockbusters, orchestras playing pop music and conductors bounding about like rock stars.*

Bill nodded. *You would make an excellent tutor, Loretta.*

Oh Bill, we've talked about this. Plenty of instructors out there. I would have no patience for tiny clumsy fingers or surly adolescents. I just want to extend the lives of players like me.

Loretta spent hours a day on the phone soliciting support from town officials and beseeching musicians to join her cause. She subsisted on vegetable smoothies boosted with protein powder, her fluid body now as taut as her bow. Rarely the dinners she once prided in presenting, more often takeout, which ended up cold on the counter, or wrapped in the refrigerator, because Bill had taken to stopping after work at a pub where residents and nurses convened at the end of day, tapping into their vitality and absorbing their optimism, but still finding it difficult to look forward. A sign, he concluded, the time for retirement was nigh. What might be next? What used to be a sense of direction, a shared path with his wife, seems now a black hole, and he fears he will have to adapt to the sobering realization that nothing will cure her resolve to establish a home for music by taking over their own home.

One night, Bill wilted into bed while Loretta was checking her last messages, she set aside the phone and turned to him to ask a question she had asked long ago, when he first decided emergency medicine was his calling.

Tell me about the ER, she asked, as she turned off her bedside lamp, his one low light enveloping them in a soft glow.

Bill answered the same way he had all those years ago, when he promised not to bring work home. A promise he has kept, making her current plan all the more paradoxical.

Truth is, little has changed, he answered. *Drug overdoses. Knife or gun wounds so deep into internal organs to cause permanent dysfunction, if they survive. Inadequate prenatal care for the poor. The elderly, vulnerable. Broken spirits with broken bones. Sepsis rampant. Occasionally, the innocuous soot in an eye, a nasty fall or a flu, but more often, the ravages of mental illness. Lost souls.*

Tears fell to Loretta's cheeks as she grasped his hand to her heart.

You are the truly exceptional, Bill.

He might have argued the point, but he understood she hoped to validate his purpose as she demanded purpose for herself.

Watching Loretta sleep that night, her bright eyes closed to him, Bill noticed that her features – balanced, pleasing – seemed, even at rest, dissonant. Beyond signs of age, the sign of discontent. The fear of losing time. She needed more than playing here and there, subject to the whims of irascible conductors. She will be her own conductor now.

Bill understood their lives will not play out as planned, but they will play out together. For better and for worse.

The town declined to permit the project.

How foolish he was, Bill realized, to imagine that would be the end of it. Loretta hired a retired urban planner to navigate the labyrinth of local planning. He counseled her to establish a non-profit, with donation-based recitals only, and valet parking to mitigate neighborhood impact. Performance days and hours were restricted, and the fire department capped capacity. To Bill's astonishment, the neighbors rallied to her side and the city gave a thumbs up to a home concert center.

The Salon on Spring Street, Loretta cried joyfully at a celebratory dinner, to the cheers of the architect and builder, the consultant, also a former member of the celebrated Lark Quartet, who had agreed to serve on the board, as well as both children and their partners, and Bill, who sat at the table's end like a coda.

She came to bed that night in a short silk nightgown and pressed her body to his, their lovemaking a resounding crescendo to lifelong hopes and plans, and on to a new denouement. Not an ending, as much as a different direction, for the foreseeable future.

On a balmy evening nearly a year to the day Loretta's plan took shape, under a cerulean blue, cloudless sky, perforated by a full moon, her string quartet presented Beethoven's *Opus 132 in A Minor*, better known as the quartet of transcendence. With Loretta as lead violin, they performed to an audience of friends and family seated in their former living room, also a smattering of local officials and supporters, their music resounding from a state of the art acoustic ceiling, out to the street to a crowd of music lovers seated on grass or chairs, sprayed by falling leaves. A night, in every way, described by an arts reporter as transcendent.

This Opus, composed in the mid-1800s during a serious illness, and nearly twice as long as his famous first symphony, evokes what aficionados consider the most soulful music Beethoven ever composed. Introduced with ominous tones, the early movements summon darkness and suffering, transitioning to a stirring, seventeen minute meditation conjuring the joy of being alive. An exultant finish echoes the opening strains, signifying joy dimmed by persistent shadows.

A perfect choice for the launch, Bill agreed, as he leaned against a wall in the foyer to listen, transported by the music and pleased for his wife.

At the close, after a standing ovation, he tried and failed to catch her eye, surrounded as she was by well-wishers. Instead, he climbed the stairs and stood very still for a moment on the landing, disoriented, as he has been for weeks, like a prowler in his own home, before making his way to their new bedroom, where his chest of drawers had been situated on a different wall and the closet carved into a passage to a new bathroom. He stripped off and spread on the bed a tuxedo Loretta rented for him, pulled on a clean shirt, khaki pants and sneakers, and one of his white physician's jackets, in response to a call for support for medical staff to deal with a fatal multi-vehicle accident.

He was glad to return to where his presence will matter.

Loretta scanned the crowd for him, while basking in the glow of approbation. She toasted sponsors and patrons with champagne, and then stepped outside to blow kisses to the neighbors, her spirits soaring with pride of accomplishment, as well as the glorious music.

When the last of well-wishers finally bid farewell, the last glasses set into caterer's boxes and chairs folded away, she stood in the silence and closed her eyes, still swaying to the strings playing in her head and filled with satisfaction, before she locked the doors, turned off all the lights, and slowly ascended the stairs in the dark, feeling her way with her fingertips on the banister as if plucking a violin.

Bill, she called out, her voice weary, eyes bleary, transcendence fading.

Bill? she repeated, curious where he can be at this hour, after this magical evening.

At the sight of what seemed a lifeless body on the bed, she gasped, and then smiled with relief when she realized it was the tuxedo, which she hung and buttoned on the hangar waiting on the closet door. Bill would return by morning. Joy faded by shadows, she thought, humming the last bars of the opus as she shed her clothes to a heap on the floor and collapsed under the duvet onto a cold bed.

Reverse Image

I saw her at Saks today. My mother. Rather, a woman who looked the way she might have looked, if she were alive. If she had been born white, instead of black.

Ridiculous, I sputtered, peering around me, sheepishly. An elder black woman, even a stately black woman, like me, muttering under her breath, might scare shoppers. I could seem scary. I may be going mad. More likely, tired. I slept very little last night and sleepless nights corrupt cognitive functions. Chronic insomnia, in fact, has been proven to induce a form of hypermania. Last night, the annual Hunter's moon illuminated the night sky, the autumn full moon closest to the equinox, its brilliance expedient for hunting prey, and also known for invoking hallucination.

Madness notwithstanding, impossible to dispute the likeness. The same heart-shaped face. High cheekbones. Shallow brow. Full lips and deep set, mahogany eyes. This woman, however, exuded serenity. Blessed with good health and longevity. A gift too often denied.

But then, I recalled the date. This day, a late September day, fifty years ago, the day my mother took her final breath. Ten years post-diagnosis, eight months after a brief remission, five days after she was admitted to the clinic for, as she predicted, the last time.

I was fifteen years old.

I should have noticed when I checked my calendar. I make note of such things, as a rule, although my older daughter admonished me, years ago, to mark birthdays, not death days.

Commemorations and celebrations only, she advised. Advice I have heeded.

I had arrived at Saks to find a special present for a friend turning seventy. A woman who professes to want nothing more than she has. *Just another year,* she protests, denying the onset of an eighth decade. I'm as lazy a shopper as we all are now, and usually scan the internet marketplace for the right gift at the right price. However, the sun was high in a powder blue sky, an autumn day surprisingly warm, so I chose instead to walk to the flagship store midtown to see and touch what I might choose, the pleasure of the tactile so rare in our cyber-commerce culture.

I first saw her, this pale version of my mother, while perusing a sea of colorful silk scarves folded under glass into a kaleidoscope of pigment and designs, like fractals, which has not crossed my mind since I retired from the research lab last year. Fractal. The word itself sounds mystical, a term popularized as I came of age, in the 70s, to define repetitive patterns in nature that replicate infinitely. In the scarf display, magnified by glass, waves of shape and color seemed dynamic, ominous, as if an orca might leap out to drag me down to the deep. When I turned away, fearfully, and looked up, there she was. My lovely, long gone mother, as if to protect me.

I was five years old when she was diagnosed with a cancer medical science had yet to decode, far too young to comprehend why she was not at home for long stretches of time, much less the abrupt dramatic shift in the tenor of conversation. The pacing of our days. The very air seemed harder to breathe. My mother, increasingly tired, agitated. My father, rarely home, working extra jobs, because even at the clinic, there were fees. Medications. And

I, an only child, trapped in a dark forest like a tree felled by lightning, the wood decaying, slowly, bit by bit, day by day.

Children feel things far more intensely than adults recognize. They sense even the most subtle alteration in the family dynamic. When my mother was admitted to the clinic for treatment, for days, sometimes a week, I stayed with an aunt who lived close by, enjoying the company of my two spirited cousins and the hearty dinners my aunt prepared, every night, no matter the fatigue of a long work day or how skimpy the ingredients on hand. After dinner, after a bath, after the nightly reading time my aunt, and my mother, required, I dozed on a couch until my father returned at midnight to scoop me up, carry me the four blocks to our apartment and deposit me onto my little bed in the corner of the room the three of us shared, so I might wake the next morning at home. I remember still the chill that swept over me as he pulled me from a dream, the strength of his embrace and the reassuring cadence of his walk, and then, after he tucked me into my cold bed, I listened for his nightly routine, waiting for my body to warm and for all the lights to go out, so I might sleep.

Being at home, where my mother would eventually return, was the comfort he meant for me. Once I turned ten, however, he insisted I walk home from my aunt's after dinner, the indoctrination to independence believed to be imperative for city kids, particularly the only child of a mother with an abbreviated lifeline, the loneliness of daily solitude rehearsal for the rest of my life.

In the 60s, cancer treatments were in infancy, a hodge-podge as sketchy as snake oil, dispensed in a facility, in my mother's case, a clinic for the poor, where physicians from city hospitals donated one day each week to share expertise and compensate for limited staff. Children under the age of sixteen were not permitted to visit; however, I was smuggled in, every Wednesday, by a soft-hearted oncologist who took an interest in my mother's case. An older white physician, nearly bald, with sloped shoulders, who was frustrated with the sloth-like progress into research to sooner diagnose the cancers too often treated too late. What he could do, for which I've always been grateful, was spare a young girl from the trauma of prolonged separation, until I could no longer be spared.

My children were teenagers the day I turned forty, the age my mother was when she died, and I recall being stricken, surprisingly for the first time, by what it must have been like for a vibrant woman to have no sense of future beyond its end. To awaken every day knowing that at any moment, perhaps without warning, she might abandon her child. Unfathomable then; frankly, still.

She was fierce, my mother. Determined to prove the primacy of mind over matter. She bore brutal treatments without a word. In fact, I saw her cry only once, in 1968, not for herself. I was eight years old, shocked to find her standing with my aunt, arms wrapped around each other, staring at a tiny TV screen, weeping for Martin Luther King. A man none of us knew, albeit known to us all. A beacon of hope, he seemed invincible, until that day, like a mother seems to a child.

It was during one of those long clinic stays when I read aloud to her from my biology textbook about fractals. I was not then a fan of the sciences, but I was a diligent student. Text books, to my restless mind, were monotonous, but to her, whose high school science classes were home economics, a paradise of wonder.

She was especially fascinated by biology, which, she said, seemed more spiritual than empirical. *A matter of faith, but unreachable without the knowledge.*

I suspect she wished for an explanation of why her own biology had failed her.

Reading to her, watching her face light up, enchanted, fostered in me a greater regard for science, and when I earned top grades, an oddity then for a girl, I found myself on a path to laboratory research, and ultimately, medical research – forty years and more trying to drill down to the sources of terminal disease, and establishing a foundation for modern targeted treatments. I spent many late nights assessing discovery research to secure grant funding to investigate why cancer is more often fatal in black people, although we know why. Less about biology, more about poverty, stress, paltry medical care and pollutants. We know.

That day, nearing her end, she listened with her eyes closed, breathing in short sighs, as I explained that fractals, which exist in a plethora of phenomena, present as recurring geometric shapes within geometric shapes.

Every fractal, every element of a fractal, regardless of the angle of observation, echoes the whole, like a visual loop, I read, and when she nodded, I clarified in words that spoke to her poetic disposition. *Like a perfectly symmetrical leaf. The unfolding petals of a rose. Shimmering crystals in morning dew.*

Oh, how she smiled at those words. She understood. And today, she would appreciate the symmetry in the doppelganger.

My mother would have been intrigued as well to know that digital algorithms rely on fractals. She would have been fascinated by modern technology, because she believed lives are shaped by what can be, more than what is, or has been. I might argue that point with her, if she were alive to argue, despite my lifelong dedication to possibilities. Then again, if she were alive, she would have made her point.

I shook my head to dispel memory and wandered an aisle toward a display of purses and stylish phone cases; however, women are fussy about what we carry with us, the odds of choosing well for someone else, small. Jewelry, far too personal, as well as expensive.

Hoping still to find the perfect gift, I ventured into the jungle of perfume, where the olfactory assault made me gasp for breath. As I turned to flee, my mother's double stood before me and I froze, again, barely breathing, watching her in profile while waiting for her to turn toward me again so I might dwell on the face I've longed to see, despite being convinced I had long ago moved beyond the longing.

The night before my mother was admitted to the clinic for the last time, I awoke at midnight. Not a rarity. I was always attuned to her sounds, as she frequently awakened in pain. That night, I heard her slip from bed and slip into her worn slippers, then tiptoe to the kitchen to brew chamomile tea. In our tiny apartment, every sound reverberated in the hush of night, the rare few hours of something like silence in the city, although she was an expert at moving through rooms like a sprite, so my father and I might sleep well and rise with the vitality she drew from us. I always stayed in bed, a blanket pulled to my chin, silently hearkening to every move she made. The stream of water from the faucet, the clink of the lid to the teapot, the bubbling boil, the moment she pulled the pot from the flame, before the shrill, then a teaspoon dipped into a honey jar, followed by a gentle stir against a porcelain cup, three times, every time. A ritual, meaning, for me, all is well, as well as can be.

When the chair squeaked against the linoleum and she sat, when I heard the first satisfying sip of the brew, I slept.

That night, however, all of a sudden, her laughter penetrated my twilight state, like lightning in a clear summer night sky. A sound exceedingly rare in her last years, the radiation, chemotherapy and steroid infusions, analgesic medications and nerve tonics, having poisoned her psyche as well as all her cells in a desperate effort to destroy the offenders.

I told them to use me like a lab rat, she explained, when she believed I was old enough to understand. *Not for me, too late for me, but someone else who might live longer because of what they learn from me.*

Her nobility was wasted on me then. I wanted my mother to live. To be cured. I cared nothing for anyone else, not then.

I let my curiosity propel me out of bed that night, tracing her hilarity to the bathroom, where she stood staring at herself in the mirror over the sink with an expression of sheer glee. She wore the pink silk nightgown and robe my father had pinched pennies to gift to her for the longer stays at the clinic, which made her seem, to me, a movie star.

When she turned to me, gripping what I could not see between thumb and forefinger, I thought she might be sleepwalking. Perhaps, hallucinating, which happened when her brain was on fire from radiation. I did my best to stay calm, praying she would not slip into a stupor, or collapse, although seeing her joyful made me joyful. Jubilance as contagious as despair.

What is it, I asked, giggling with her.

She put a finger to her lips to shush us. *A gray hair. A real gray hair*, she whispered.

A nearly invisible gray strand. One tiny emblem of age, particularly in black women who tend to gray later. Just as black skin stays smooth longer, what my aunt called *black don't crack* skin. Small recompense for the indignities otherwise imposed.

I moved closer, squinting to see. *A wavy gray hair*, I whispered, and we both chuckled, because after a second round of chemotherapy, after losing all her thick jet black hair, her hair grew back wavy rather than coiled to her scalp, which she proclaimed a reward for endurance.

Imagine that! she cried out with laughter as new hair emerged. *Maybe my skin will turn coal black next time*, she cackled to my aunt, whose skin, like mine, was two shades darker than my mother's mocha, what my aunt called *paper bag black*, a historical offense, but a source of good-natured teasing between them.

In a black and white photo, she might have been mistaken for a woman with olive skin, like her lookalike at Saks.

Her death, weeks after the discovery of that small sign of age, was particularly cruel. A moment of joy crushed by a disease I pictured then as an alien piercing her organs, like the wildly popular *Invasion of the Body Snatcher* films. The aliens won.

She was old before her time, never old.

At Saks, as I stared at her reverse image, I reminded myself that this white woman was an imitation, not a replica, although very close. So close, I could not turn my eyes away, as she lifted a small white card from a pile at the Chanel counter, these meant to spray and wave before the nose to capture the fragrance. She frowned at the first, smiled at the next, and then, disinterested, moved on.

I followed in her footsteps and when she paused to answer her phone, I stood nearby, hidden by a column, to study her closely, like a slide under a microscope. Shockingly she also had a tiny cleft in her gently pointed chin, the cleft I tried to swipe away when I was a child, like a smudge of chocolate frosting. One of many childhood games we played, games she also played with my cousins or the neighbor's children, because my mother was a playful person at heart and, for this reason, we knew at once, my father and I, when the pain was excruciating or when remission was coming to an end. She retreated then from play, and from most everyone, except me.

Hard to guess this woman's age, but I imagine she's older than I by a decade or more, and aging well – spine erect, head high on a graceful neck, skin smooth at the cheekbones, wrinkles relegated to the lips and eyes, along the jaw. She wore merely a dusting of make-up, enough to appear fresh rather than faded, and I could not restrain a smile at her lush silver hair, brushed back from her face. She wore stylish clothes in rich fall colors, and black leather boots with a low heel, as if she had stepped out of *Harper's Bazaar*, a magazine my mother perused weekly at the library, searching every page for signs of the good life. Searching, I believe, for a small sign of herself, if destiny had been kind.

She was a sickly child, a frail adolescent.

Married at twenty-two, a mother at twenty-five, and by thirty, the prime of life, her body under assault. She had a taste for hearty food, but a humble appetite, so painfully thin when in treatment I felt the daggers of her ribs when she hugged me before I left for school, and again, when I returned, and the precious tight embrace at bedtime, as if she might not see the dawn. I've wondered over the years if she feared never seeing me again each time I left the house as much as I feared the loss of her from sleep to daylight, and then, on the walk home from school, the near paralyzing fear of her lifeless body on the other side of the door.

Many mornings, awakened early by the relentless alarm, resenting the start of the day, the chores to complete before rushing off to school, I would find my mother curled up on the couch, wrapped in a blanket like a cocoon, a library book having slipped to the floor and an empty tea cup on the coffee table. An impressionist painting, rendered by a Harlem Renaissance artist, depicting a fraught black woman in a rare moment of tranquility.

I was twelve when she acknowledged to me she would be gone sooner than later, when death became my rival, having been something like mythos before. She insisted, however, she planned to hang on long enough to greet her grandchildren, her optimism maddening in its madness.

I will not have children, I decided in that moment, as if to punish her. Why would I reward her with a second generation to abandon? But then, when the time was right, I cherished my children all the more.

Now, all these years later, her reflection stands before me, maternal wine in a stranger's cask, and I feel, as I felt then, but could not express, how cruel the legacy of loss.

I attended a conference some years ago, where the wife of a colleague gave a talk about motherless children. They are called semi-orphans if the other parent is present, and there is no greater trauma for a child than to lose a mother, even a bad parent, she reported, referring to children removed from drug-addicted or abusive parents. My mother was a loving mother, struggling to stay alive, and, I was well prepared for her death, if we are ever prepared. I don't think of myself as orphaned, or traumatized, rather lost, missing, as if my hand slipped from her grip in a crowded train station, and I was never reclaimed.

I shadowed her facsimile like a spy, from perfume to cosmetics, where she dabbed blush to her cheeks and shadow to her eyelids, tilting her face to a mirror with a smile, adjusting a silk scarf that wrapped her neck and draped to her breasts, its fringes swaying as she walked. Hot tears pressed behind my eyes as I strained to hold them back, if only so my vision would not blur. I followed her as she strolled aisle to aisle, watching her halt at a display of shawls, fabrics and colors woven together like a patchwork quilt, her fingers tenderly grazing the cloth, until she sauntered to Couture. My mother would have liked to dress stylishly. *Champagne taste on a beer budget,* she would say, with an aggrieved smirk. Now and then, my aunt sewed her a frock from a pattern matching an elegant image in a fashion magazine, which would hang like a trophy in the closet.

I trailed her to an elevator, desperate to hear her speak. Photographs last, images linger in memory, but a voice is forever silenced, even in dreams. I stood so close I could have touched her. I could have gripped the hem of her skirt, like a child. As the doors closed, she stepped back to make room for me, to expand the distance between us. She must have known I was following her and she may have sensed my nearly desperate need to connect. Or, she may have felt uneasy in enclosed space so near a black woman who may be unhinged. I did not acknowledge her move, rather stood, stiff and silent, until the doors opened, when I stepped aside for her to go ahead, to which she nodded, and then I tracked her footsteps to the lounge, where she stayed a few moments in a stall, and when she emerged, she glanced at me without a smile or a comment, turning her back to wash her hands and refresh her lipstick at the mirror.

Flower petal pink on warm, atypically plump lips.

I can still feel my mother's kiss on my cheek, the lipstick circle left behind, another game we played, although there was no need for lipstick to leave her mark.

The woman turned to me at last with a curious expression. There you are, sweetheart, she might have said, as if I had merely been misplaced. She granted me only a baffled half-smile, and when I took a step in her direction, she stiffened. She must have seen the fury in my eyes, the anger withheld so long.

Perhaps she sensed the threat of a woman maddened by a Hunter's moon.

Where have you been? I silently cried. Where were you the years I crept through adolescence like a shadow of myself? When I graduated college, the first of the family line. When my greed for affection was so severe I bungled one relationship after another, and ruined my marriage. When my daughters were born with your eyes, the elder with your smile. Where were you the day I found my first gray hair? I screamed internally, tears raining down my cheeks.

The woman stood, perfectly composed, not moving a muscle, as if I were a mountain lion who might pounce at the first sign of fear.

Have no fear of me, I should have said. You are no more than a stand-in and I am not dangerous, even if I seem so.

I sighed then, exasperated with myself as well as with my long gone mother, and the woman must have recognized the sorrow in the sigh, as her expression softened.

Something I can do for you, dear?

I forced a wan smile, swiping tears from my cheeks. *Sorry, you remind me of someone.*

She sighed, with obvious relief.

Ah, I see. Someone important? she asked.

I nodded.

People say I look like Lena Horne.

Lena Horne? I bellowed.

Well, yes, I know, seems strange, but I've been compared to her. An older version, of course.

My mother would never be so arrogant to compare herself to a celebrity! I shouted, my voice menacing with outrage. *She was humble in her beauty, which made her all the more beautiful.*

I felt the adrenaline pulse through my veins, like the first dose of a narcotic, and my blood pressure, chronically high, elevated, my body overcome by the fight or flight instinct, even as I stood immobilized in her presence.

Oh, I see. Your mother, she murmured, kindly, despite her furrowed brow. A white woman compared to a light-skinned celebrity seems plausible, but likened to a dark-skinned woman? Confusing, for sure. *Never easy to lose a mother,* she said, sympathetically, perhaps to engage me in a conversation I would not have with a stranger, resemblance notwithstanding.

I stared at her, sadly now, and she stood her ground, staring back, but with compassion, inciting further fury, as I would rather apathy. However kind a sympathetic gesture is meant to be, it is a reflection, an indictment, of pity, which my mother would not have sanctioned. And I am my mother's daughter.

We stood, like desperados at a shootout, until she sighed deeply, unfolded a black jacket hanging over one arm and slipped it on, one sleeve, then another, buttoning, slowly, to defy the ominous stranger by declaring she was not one to fade in the face of conflict. Yet another trait she shared with my mother: poise.

She nodded then, not for permission, or in commiseration, rather confirming an end to the confrontation. She must have been afraid to be cloistered again in the elevator, so she climbed the stairs, with noticeable effort, tight joints I imagine, and she must have been aware of me following a few steps behind, but she kept going, without glancing back. At the top, she paused to take a deep breath, and then she glided across the grand foyer to the main entrance and through the revolving doors to the street. From the serenity of Saks to the bustling shelter of Fifth Avenue.

I huddled near the doorway like a child playing hide and seek, watching as she raised one arm, as gracefully as a dancer, two fingers held aloft until a taxi lurched to a stop, when she stepped off the curb, opened the yellow door and slid in, slamming the door behind her. I kept my eyes on her silhouette in the rear window, until the taxi blended into the sea of taxis shrouded in kinetic traffic, and then, until faded to a speck in the distance. The mixture of shapes, colors, motion, melded into a fractal, its elements splitting repeatedly like the ripples of a pebble on a pond, into what seems the same, but is never precisely the same.

Like the spirit, my mother would have said. Forever present, in whatever form.

Neither With nor Without

Late one night, that hour when stillness and darkness cloak the sleepless, and when an aching heart silences reason, Angie posted to what she still thinks of as Twitter.

The days are long, the nights are cold. I miss you, still.

As a rule, Angie is not one to speak from the heart, certainly not on social media. She's a tenured history professor. A scholar. Serious about word and deed. For the sake of networking, and natural curiosity, she follows, and has a small following, of fellow historians, as well as a handful of eccentric intellectuals. She reads the daily missives from Heather Cox Richardson, in awe of her ability to synthesize past and current events in real time. She has a longstanding crush on physicist Neil deGrasse Tyson and the philosopher Maria Popova. She begrudgingly acknowledges that social media serves, now and then, as a distraction from the drudgery of lesson plans or indolent students. Still, she shudders at the hyperbolic comments and is often nearly apoplectic at the prevalence of misinformation.

What was that? her friend Joyce asked, when she called the following morning.

Joyce calls early mornings, sometimes again late afternoons, because Angie, naturally reclusive, has bordered on hermitic since she split with Alex, three months ago.

What was what?

That tweet. X, horrid name, horrid space. Have you been taken over by aliens?

Very funny.

Still makes me sad. Still makes me mad.

Joyce introduced Angie to Alex and she takes her friend's broken heart personally.

All good things come to an end and they were the best two years of my life, Angie said.

Until they weren't, Joyce replied.

Yes, but first they were, Angie insisted.

A few days later, in the light of day, in yet another atypically impulsive state of mind, Angie shared a similar sentiment to Facebook, which she reserves for a small cadre of mostly childhood friends and long-distance family. She rarely posts, and only what she would not fear being noticed by a student or a colleague, and she will occasionally click a thumbs up to feign interest, despite a lack of interest in the plethora of self-indulgent, self-congratulatory postings and comments, the parade of political tirades and false narratives and, her least favorite of all, pet videos.

He might notice the Facebook, Joyce said.

Do they have a share only with ex's option?

If they don't, they will.

A designation for the great romance?

You're joking, but they are cutting this pie so fine, they might. Whatever he is…

Was… Angie interjected.

I still follow him, just to know what he's up to, Joyce confessed.

I'm quite certain he unfollowed me, Angie said. *I bet he blocked me.*

Don't think we will ever be friends, Alex snarled, as he charged out the door the day he moved out.

Alex is the man Angie believed was the love of her life. They met in their sixties, well beyond failed marriages and identity crises. Children on their own paths. Careers winding down and IRA accounts intact. They pledged forever, they were certain of it, which made the breakup all the more unfathomable.

Maybe I do better on my own, she cried to

Alex that fateful day. *I'm worn out. I need time to recalibrate,* she wailed, in a voice even she didn't recognize, which Alex would describe, in one of a series of scathing texts, as a screech. *Like a crow and just as murderous.*

She should have seen it coming. Her last book died on the vine and a year of research into another went nowhere. Her finances were stretched tighter than usual, so in addition to her university course load, she took on writing textbook chapters she had hoped by this point in her career to avoid. When her daughter, who lived seventy miles south, had a third child, Angie shorted her class schedule to help. Twice a week, early morning, she transported the five year old to kindergarten, constructed puzzles and read books with the toddler, and after pickup, took them both for snacks at a kid-friendly coffee house, so her daughter might sleep when the baby napped. In the afternoons, while the boys rested, she walked the newborn around the neighborhood in the stroller, and when she dozed, Angie sat on a bench checking emails and phone messages. Late afternoon, she washed and folded laundry, unloaded the dishwasher, and packed up toys and books into their bins. She chatted with her son-in-law when he returned from work, before the long drive back, often stuck in traffic, and wobbling dangerously, now and then, until she arrived home, so tired she had little leftover for Alex, who had been besieged for months with a slipped disk that would require surgery.

Sheer madness, that's what it was. Like something out of Ibsen, Angie cried to Joyce a few days after the split. *I used to be more resilient.*

I'm so sorry I didn't realize how bad it was then, Joyce said.

I never want to be a women who rants.

Ranting is essential, Joyce responded.

This may be the closest thing to a breakdown I've had. Do they even call them breakdowns now?

Not nervous breakdowns, too 60s.

There must be a DSM designation between heartbreak and psychotic break, Angie argued.

Check into that, please, and let me know. I'm planning a breakdown myself one of these days, Joyce said, with a laugh.

A pastry chef with a thriving bakery, Joyce breaks down ingredients to a molecular level, like a chemist, reconstructing into the delectable. The most grounded woman Angie knows. *You're a rock,* Angie said. *A boulder in fact. You would never crumble the way I did.*

All that chocolate keeps me giddy.

Chocolate therapy would be divine, if I had an appetite, Angie grumbled.

My dear, you hit a wall. Going in too many directions. No wonder you wore down, Joyce said.

We blew up like a dust storm, Angie said.

Not since Angie was a teaching assistant and divorced mother of two young children, has she felt so inadequate. She found herself trembling in the middle of the day, muscles as sore as if she'd been mountain climbing, then sinking into sleep on the couch in the middle of a movie, or apologetically crawling to bed to sleep like the dead, then waking with a start when Alex, a night owl, slipped in and curled his body to her, and again, a few hours later, for the first of his hot showers, after which she massaged medicinal cream to his spine.

A menthol scent saturated her fingertips for months, ameliorated only some by baby oil.

Angie, I'm sure you're still beating yourself up, you do that. Maybe he is too, Joyce pondered.

More likely licking his wounds, Angie said.

Pay attention to the filling, not the glaze, my friend, Joyce advised.

On reflection, she would admit, only to Joyce, *if I had been calmer, he would have been more rational. He might have heard what I was saying between the lines. When I blew, he blew, and then I shut down. I could have done a better job explaining my feelings, but I needed him to get it, without working so hard for it. Is that too much to ask?*

Talk to someone, Joyce suggested. *I mean a shrink or a doctor.*

Done. Low on iron. I'm emotionally anemic. And Alex has a tender heart.

He wounds easily, sure, but don't we all? Joyce countered.

Yes, but the constant pain, the client stress, Angie argued in his defense.

She could have been more sympathetic. He could have been more understanding. They may have been headed for a cliff all along.

All for the best, Alex declared in the end. *I guess we're not meant to be forever after all.*

Every relationship has a hidden fault line, this much Angie knows, so she knows she should have paid attention to the rumbling. Neither was he. And that, was that.

How often has she heard women repeat that old saying they cannot live with the men they love and cannot live without them. Still, some, many, work through conflict. They don't bolt when it's too hard, only when untenable, which is why Angie fled her marriage. They had married young – graduate students who mistook infatuation for love. He was a stoner. She, a striver. They had to pinch pennies. Two children were born too soon, and with them, the last gasp of romantic idealism. When he left, clinging to the caution that those who cannot remember the past are condemned to repeat it, Angie avoided relationships. She rationalized that if it were meant to be, it would not be hard. All these years later, with Alex, the corollary raised its ugly head: too good to be true may be too good to last.

She raised her children. She focused on publication and tenure. She had a small, solid circle of friends, and the stimulus of students. She enjoyed the casual sexual encounter. She convinced herself she had what she needed.

And then, in a random, life-altering moment, she met Joyce at a local café for lunch, and Alex was lunching with a colleague of her husband. When they were introduced, Alex removed his sunglasses, and peered at her with the penetrating gaze and warm smile of a man with passion. He stood to shake her hand. Tall and lean, when he spoke, his gravelly voice syncopated like a sacred chant.

She was entranced, at once.

When Joyce said Angie teaches history, Alex crooned from the Sam Cooke song, *don't know much about history. Although,* he said, a sparkle in his hazel eyes, *I'm good at geography.*

Angie laughed, the ring of her laughter as surprising and pleasing as the attraction.

When Joyce groaned she was starving, Angie handed Alex her card. *Should you wish a history lesson,* she said, and he nodded, with a knowing smile.

He called three days later. He had taken the time to read her last book before the call. When she told Joyce she was touched, Joyce laughed. *That's called foreplay, my friend.*

They spent weekends together at his place or hers for six months before he moved into Angie's cottage. They squeezed their stuff in as best they could, insisting it was cozy, not cramped. Their circadian rhythms lined up. They ate the same foods, preferred the same wines. They liked each other's friends, who all agreed they were perfect for each other. Seated close at cafés and coffee shops, they brushed shoulders. In movie theaters, they held hands. Strangers remarked on their amorous glow.

I feel young again, she told her children.

I wake up smiling. Whatever comes next is fine.

It was not fine, in the end.

Two days after the first tweet, Angie posted again…

Stuck between the proverbial rock and hard place. Like that old familiar saying – can't live with you, can't live without you. I thought it was a foolish cliché. I get it now.

She scolded herself for succumbing to the worst of pop culture and focused on work. Midterms to grade. Faculty planning meetings. Research for an article she was asked to write about Wassily Kandinsky in the years leading to the Russian revolution. A proponent of the avant-garde, his abstracted art conflicted with the communist directive to the utilitarian.

One night, again in the wee hours, she tied the artist to Alex in a tweet…

Kandinsky, an aesthetic theorist, hoped to liberate painting from its ties to traditional imagery. He depicted images based on what he called inner necessity. You made me believe I was your inner necessity. An abstraction, I see. #abstractart #Kandinsky

The next night, after another sleepless night, she was scanning information on other expressionists for context and posted again…

Rothko, Russian born, is best known for color blocks evoking apathy, or passivity, until you look closely. Layers of angst in layers of paint. The surreal masked in serenity. I stare at them and weep. Were we so saturated we were surreal? #abstractexpressionism #Rothko

A week later, Angie ran into a colleague who contends gossip is essential narrative. He once confessed he reads *People* magazine at the library, boasting that he would never stoop to a subscription. *The content is history in the making,* he has argued in his defense.

I hear Alex has moved on, he said, with a cunning smile. *A philanthropist, I've met her at university events. Attractive. Smart, too. I guess he has a type. And you? Back out there yet?*

Angie could barely breathe, unwilling to reveal her shock and inclined to spit in his officious face. *Some of us don't transfer affection so easily,* she snapped.

She should not have been surprised. Alex was not the sort of man to be alone long, although he said, from the first, she was the woman he was looking for all his life.

Enraged, dejected, she tweeted...

You said I was the one you waited for. The most interesting woman you ever met.

You showered me with affection. Your last love, you said. How quickly I've been replaced.

The next morning, when Angie picked up the phone, groggy from yet another restless night, Joyce said, *your tweets have been noticed.*

Her posts had been re-tweeted, mostly between strangers, with many new followers.

Welcome to the insanely voyeuristic world of social media, Joyce chuckled.

Angie's editor surprised her later in the day with a phone call. *Launch a blog constructed around those tweets,* she announced, in lieu of hello. *Post daily. Build a fan base. Might be a book in this. A historical study of ill-fated romance?*

The editor is one of a rare breed devoted to scholarly material, but always on the hunt for more commercial projects to subsidize the highbrow. Angie pictured her at her oversized mahogany desk – thick glasses slipping to the tip of her nose, shoulders and spine curled to piles of manuscripts in cardboard boxes, like miniature coffins. Pop rock bands play in the background, just loud enough to feel the beat, which Angie found an endearing contradiction the first time they met, and since. She imagined her flipping pages, a sharp pencil in one hand, while expounding vociferously on blogging, the last thing Angie ever expected to hear from this champion of the intellectual.

A blog? This is personal, Angie argued. *Frankly, I don't know what came over me.*

A good blog is the modern equivalent of the diaries and letters you scholars cherish for source material. Personal expression in the details, right? Elizabeth Barrett and Robert Browning. Scott and Zelda. Hamilton! Talk about riches. A biography, a musical! Angie, there's gold in this, she barked, and hung up.

Angie stared at the phone in her hand as if a grenade. *Madness,* she muttered.

Beyond the book reviews or profiles of historical figures Angie writes, primarily for additional income, she has, in the last decade, edited an anthology of essays on gothic literature, and a biography of George Eliot focused on the historical context of her fiction. Neither sold out their first printing. Her agent, a no-nonsense, foul-mouthed Brit, the only agent years ago to take a chance on the young scholar, and who battles for her writers like a boxer, has been on Angie's case since to come up with something marketable.

When Angie called to report the editor's prompt, the agent turned up the heat. *Fucking brilliant! Right, you don't want to become another brainiac who falls to the wayside. Think of a blog as sharpening your literary pencil.*

Angie laughed, the first genuine laugh she's had in months. *To put the words literary and blog in the same sentence is oxymoronic.*

Don't be such a snob, the agent retorted. *There are fantastically creative blogs out there. And fabulous musings of the inquiring mind. Vivian Gornick. Teju Cole. Maggie Nelson. Patti Smith has had a renaissance. Literary flaneurs. Think big!*

I'm a historian, I'm all about past tense, Angie argued.

Historians use the lessons of the past to explain the present, right? Flip it. Use the present to illuminate the past. Weave them together more intricately. Intimately, I should say. The culture of romance. Romance in culture. Spread your wings, Angie. Make magic!

Ridiculous, Angie grumbled.

Make magic? She barely has energy to meet her deadlines, consumed with what went wrong with Alex. Forever exhuming the past, to make sense of the nonsensible, while Alex dealt only with what was in front of him until smacked in the head, rarely looking back other than to lick his wounds.

He told her once the most important thing to him was to speak truth in real time. Angie, however, is a researcher. She prefers to mull things over, figure things out, gather her thoughts. Contemplation yields revelation, she tells students. If she'd been thoughtful the day she wailed to Alex that she was falling apart, they might not be here. Then again, he let her go without argument. Out the door and now, on to someone else.

We were doomed, she told Joyce then, after she'd hibernated for several days. *Maybe I'm well out of it. He was chaos in motion. He managed his life the way he made the bed – pitching the sheet and blanket over the mattress and tossing the pillows sloppily on top. No folds, no tuck.*

Angie, men don't do beds. Some things are just what they are.

She wondered, often, what would she say if she ran into Alex. He would likely ignore her, or worse, acknowledge her, cordially, as if they'd never been a couple. As if they'd never merged their bodies as one, night after night. Showered together mornings. She's no more than a wrinkled sheet now. If he noticed the posts, he would not make contact, she was sure of that. Pride takes precedence.

How did they get here? They were so madly in love.

Before she knew it, she had several hundred followers and marveled at the crazy state of a world in which intimacy is equated with anonymity. Why not blog? she wondered.

What have you got to lose? Joyce asked.

I suppose, Angie murmured.

On the other hand, she thought, what's to be gained?

Be bold. At the very least, might counter the inertia, Joyce urged.

Reason enough, Angie replied.

Thus, Angie the scholar, historian and professor, became a lovelorn blogger.

Methodical to the extreme, she first had to decide where to write the blog. A separation of labors, in effect, she has always required. She researches and sketches the first drafts of text chapters at the university library, then edits at an antique desk under a window in the back room doubling as guestroom and den. In the corners of the room, mounds of Amazon boxes overflow with rubber-banded index cards, like trash bags yet to be tossed. She writes original material at a café, ostensibly to summon the literary muses.

She decides to pen the blog at her dining table, as if to insulate the profound from the prosaic. The worn pine farm table separates the kitchen from the living room, seating for six, eight if squeezed, although she cannot recall the last time she hosted a dinner. The table has been laden for some time with research books and binders, vestiges of projects run aground, like an abandoned construction site, which she stacked on two chairs before wiping down the tabletop, then laid a placemat on one end for her laptop and a new notepad. She filled a glass with sparkling water, squeezed in a wedge of lime and licked the tart juices from her fingers, before she sat to write. She stared at the screen, dumbfounded, having no clue how to begin, so she slipped back into scholar and opened first Substack, then Medium, to examine templates: history blogs, literary blogs, art and travel. She lost two hours engrossed in a philosophy blog before she found a blog about how to construct a blog. Know your audience, the first caution. She knows that. But who is she writing for? Stay on topic, was the other salient advice, but she had yet to zero in on the real topic. Title the blog and organize content like chapters. Post thumbnails on social media.

All good advice, but a lot to manage, she thought.

How will she segment or label or format the longings of the heart?

She crawled into bed in defeat, slept like dead weight and awoke at dawn with renewed determination, like Joan of Arc.

I can do this, she murmured throughout the day, as she typed whatever came to mind, an uncommonly amorphous endeavor. The more she scribbled, the more she bled words, ending up with a rambling polemic. Okay, she thought. I'm a synthesizer. I can start with this. Refine it into nuggets, economical and punchy.

She told Joyce on the late day call she felt like one of the beat generation, freethinkers who sprawled on floor pillows at café's, in vans or flop houses, spinning thought into words the way Rumpelstiltskin spun straw into gold.

Keep it personal, Joyce advised.

Right, yes, she agreed, although hesitant to fully expose this particular personal.

That night it all came to her. She decided the best form for the blog would be epistolary, harkening to the historical letters the editor alluded to. An abbreviated correspondence, like social media postings.

She titled the site accordingly and then added a subtitle in a nod to the Victorian poets.

Letters to a Lost Love. *A Lament.*

On the home page sidebar, meant for credentials or affinity, she wrote: blog is short for weblog, a technology file as a journal. In the 19th century, however, a blog meant a servant boy, likely the origin of the term *bloke*, also a verb used by schoolboys to mean a trouncing. I begin this blog trounced by love.

#1. I miss you most at night. You kept the bed warm, you kept me warm. The heater, you called yourself, and I looked forward to that moment of bliss when you curled your body to me, your long legs enveloping mine, lips pressed to my neck. The sublime intimacy that makes sleeping with another person so grand. And then, often, in the middle of the night, in the midst of a deep sleep, you would awaken me by tugging my hips toward you until no air between us. Closer, you whispered, pulling me so tightly I had to coil into a fetal position. You'd be snoozing again in minutes, while I lay in a stupor for a time, awakening groggy and stiff. You woke smiling, chipper, reaching for your phone to check, LinkedIn, email and breaking news. I took naps now and then to make up for lost sleep. I'm not a great sleeper anyway and of late, I sleep in short spurts, even if unencumbered, greeted by the blank slate of first light and the prospect of another long day. My back no longer aches, only my heart.

The next afternoon she posted again, the brevity and freeform sentiment more satisfying than she imagined.

#2. I miss those late mornings I returned from an early class and you were still sitting on the couch, your laptop on your lap, CNN on television, breakfast dishes in the sink, and a half cup of curdling coffee on the side table, because you rarely finish while hot, the scent lingering like perfume, as you hustled to get a report ready for a meeting, because you still operate as if cramming for a final exam, smart enough to get away with it until the inevitable moment you hit a snag, followed by angry cursing at the internet or the client, something or someone in your way, the way you mutter at what you call the morons on the freeway who slow you down when you veer across two lanes to make an exit you knew was ahead. Why move slowly when you can dash? You filled my little home with the energy it was lacking although, in truth, I was relieved at times when I returned home after you were out and I could enjoy the embrace of stillness. You never understood how much I require regular detachment from the stranglehold of this busy, demanding world that wears me out. You took it personally. It was not you, it was me. Mostly.

#3. Remember when I confessed to you I'm especially frisky around a full moon? You might say I have missed you most four cycles now. I miss the lovemaking. I miss your touch. Our bodies fit so well. Your libido, which you insisted was desire for me, perpetually on high, like an adolescent in a constant state of arousal, and we behaved like teenagers, didn't we? Making out in the car. Nuzzling on banquettes at music clubs. I was high on it all, but I feared I might never satisfy you, not in any way, even though you told me you loved me, every day. And, every day, I wanted to make up for all the women who disappointed you, a tall order as it turned out. What did you want to do for me?

The next night, when she went online to craft the next post, the blog like oxygen, or an antidepressant, 650 people had viewed the first two and she had 1226 followers on Twitter.

She posted every day, venting despair,

exorcising demons, sharing heartbreak with an invisible throng of sympathetic followers. And then she took the expert's advice and tweeted to announce new posts…

I understand now when people say they crashed and burned. To crash is hard enough. We burned, a highly combustible relationship. You're the embers. I'm the ash.

Two weeks passed. She kept going. She was hooked.

#15. Profession of love is grand. You always made my heart swell. On the other hand, as it is said, talk is cheap. I wish you had inquired more often what I was working on, or reading, or thinking for that matter, as if only the moments we shared were significant, and nothing otherwise mattered to you. I pestered you with questions about what was on your mind, your family history, all of it. I learned all about your childhood and the years before we met, the highs and the lows. We ate when you were hungry and slept when you were tired. When I was away, visiting family or at a conference, when I called to describe a panel, or a museum exhibit, you listened the way a busy parent attends a toddler's tale, distracted by the day slipping away, although you always said you missed me and I'm sure you meant it. At the same time, you were easily threatened by anyone who captured my attention. Remember when I discovered the Colombian writer Juan Gabriel Vasquez? The unmagical realist, he calls himself, he blends the historical and political seamlessly in his novels. I admire his talent. Instead of reading his work, you said you were jealous of my writer-crush. I laughed it off. If I was your last love, and you mine, why that nonsense? A writer, not a stranger at a bar. Was it possible to reassure you sufficiently to trust me? In the end, of course, I let you down. Like all the others. News flash: you let me down too.

That night, another 2358 signed on to her social media, and nearly as many new blog subscribers, including someone who claimed to be Juan Gabriel Vasquez, and when she checked his profile photo, looked a lot like him.

Every night, she typed, she spewed, she resisted self-editing, and she wept.

#22. I miss you the most when sunset streams into the living room and the end of day settles the dust of the day, especially when you had a good day, when you chatted exuberantly about a project or a former client who'd made contact. Sometimes, strumming your guitar, the music my meal prep soundtrack, when you weren't flipping channels searching for the news of the day or the sport of the season. You were pleased to be my gourmet guinea pig, you called it. Remember the Peruvian ceviche? As good as anything you'd ever had, you praised. The green curry? Just spicy enough for you, not too spicy for me. All those autumn root vegetable soups? Or, when we were both beat, happy hours at bistro bars sharing small plates of food, so when we kissed, we tasted the same. These days, I have no desire to cook. I dine on carrot sticks with hummus or bowls of cereal, disinterested in anything more filling. My taste buds are also wretched.

Joyce pronounced during the next day's phone call that all relationships are a work in progress, including a long marriage like hers. *I love my boy, as you know, but sometimes I would like to push him into a wall. Or wave a wand and make him disappear. There's no there, there, Angie.*

Gertrude Stein, Angie muttered.

What?

That's her quote, about her hometown.

Well, love is a hometown, but in a constant state of transition. Relationships require regular restoration. You have to stay current. Men are only half the problem. Women can do better. It's our nature to nurture, but we have to speak our minds, and yes, we have to choose our words, the right tone of voice. That's communication 101. I don't forgive Alex for being insular. However, I fear you let the water rush the damn. Soul-searching for the blog is cathartic, but it takes two to tango, my friend, and blogging is a solo sport.

Angie spent the night replaying the two years with Alex in her mind as if she might have a Eureka moment. By morning, haggard and crestfallen, fumbling around the kitchen making coffee strong enough to jumpstart the day, she got a message from the agent urging her to use SEO to attract the algorithms. A few hours later, as if ordained, one of her most eager graduate students stopped by her office to offer to work with Angie on the blog.

As a research project, she suggested.

What do you know about SEO keywords? Angie asked.

On it, she said, with a knowing smile, and within a week, and steadily thereafter, day after day, the number of followers increased exponentially, startling Angie into wondering what she will accomplish other than building a platform for a book. Are her posts meaningful, do they have value, or just another outraged human? She should shut down, she thought. Get off this treadmill. Then again, there seemed still too much to say, and too many listening.

#34. When friends ask what happened between us, I say life got in our way. A rapid-fire series of events that left us breathless – from the rush of passion into the cauldron of emotional and physical overload. Too much in too short a period of time. Think about it. We had just moved in together when your father died, and then a favorite colleague of mine succumbed to cancer nearly overnight. An important client of yours pulled out, then another project was delayed a year, so you had to dip into your reserves. I'm always stressed about money. Then all those late night trips to the emergency room before your back surgery, nursing you in recovery at the same time I was being granny twice a week for my daughter. Not so much a perfect storm as a steady rain that seeped into a foundation not well sealed.

At the graduate student's urging, she abbreviated every blog post with a tweet and a link and added hashtags: #letterstoalostlove #lament #lostlove #lastlove #brokenhearted

#heartbroken #truelove

The agent left her a voicemail. *Readers are riveted. Have you read the comments? Other than the usual nut jobs, people are rooting for you. Seize the day, Angie. A tremendous opportunity has fallen into your lap. Don't let it go.*

Apparently, Angie realized, she has a reputation for not holding on to what matters.

She hadn't thought to read comments and was shocked by how many there were. Should she answer? She asked the student.

Silence is better. Very Elena Ferrante, she replied. *Let followers dialogue with each other. Engagement feeds the algorithm.*

Angie cannot fathom the consolation so many people take in a regurgitation of private matters. Why do hordes of strangers follow the longings of a sad older woman? An ordinary human being attempting to make sense of something beyond her faculty, although, given the response, maybe not so ordinary. Maybe the editor was right. Maybe what she has to say has relevance for those in similar straits.

She read through comments, most from women, older and younger, and all ethnicities, from mostly English speaking countries. Occasionally, a male tried to explain masculine behavior, or defend Alex, although these too seemed to be yearning for something they might cling to without fear of losing their grip.

She entered lots of thumbs up, and then tweeted…

What an amazing world we live in, to connect anonymously in personal longing with a throng of the longing.

The numbers of followers swelled. The powers that be at Substack took notice and re-stacked one of her posts. The agent grew giddy with the prospect of a book contract.

Angie sits at the dining table every night astonished and exhilarated, fully aware of the sensual satisfaction of rendering raw emotion into meaning. No, she's not writing for a book contract. Not for followers or tweeters. Nor is she writing to detox, which Joyce suggested. She is writing to Alex. She is writing to say what she could not or would not put into words, although, she knows, too little too late.

She tweets that night…

You told everyone you finally found the right woman. I felt the same. Shame on us for letting go without a fight. Yes, I slipped away. You should have held on. You could have been our anchor. You took the joy with you.

One night, staring at the laptop screen, she's again fearful of the exposure. She would not want to be dubbed a pathetic old professor. She needs to get a grip. She's an academic, not a romantic. Surely not a social media mogul. She switches gears to work on a book review nearing deadline. She lasts two days. The blog reaches out its arms to her like a lover and she surrenders.

I am impatient, you know, she muttered to Joyce on the morning call.

So? The most productive people I know are impatient.

In business, sure. In a relationship, no. Intolerance is antithetical to productivity.

Listen, intolerant means, technically, you cannot accept what you cannot tolerate.

I never wanted to hurt his feelings.

So you broke his heart.

Angie cringed at this truth.

Maybe better explained by baking, as most things are, Joyce said. *Right now, I have lemon blueberry loaves in the oven. The timer is set. I've made this cake a hundred times. Overcooked is dry. Undercooked, mushy. It's the perfect balance I'm looking for. If anything is perfect, baked goods can be. If I keep checking, I'm impatient. No harm done.*

However, if I take them out of the oven when the timer goes off, even if the toothpick inserted does not come out clean, they're ruined. No going back.

Angie turned their conversation into a blog post.

#40. We were both impatient with each other. Impatient by nature, both of us. Push-pull. You push, I pull away. Flight or fight. You fight, I take flight. You wound, I soothe. I wound, I sulk. Both of us intolerant. You will not tolerate anything you feel is threatening, and you take most things that way. We're both critical, too often, judgmental, yes, and when we were equally critical of maddening human behavior, we laughed. People are idiots, you would cry, so often true. Then again, between the two of us, we have nearly 280 IQ points. How could we be so stupid? So inflexible? Impatience is anathema to love, and war. Napoleon charging ahead too soon. Disastrous results. Begs the question, again and again, were we meant to be, or not?

Comments piled up and Angie scanned them at dinner. She graduated from hummus to veggie burgers and indulged a fondness for French wine, while reading bizarre statements people post in a frantic effort at empathy. She took evening walks after dinner, and while she walked, instead of listening to music or a book, she thought about all those suffering losses, disappointment, and how what she is writing reverberates. She marveled at her thousands of subscribers, impressed with the power of the medium, although not so different from story serializations by Dickens or Conan Doyle.

She reverted to historian.

#41. Serialized fiction proliferated in the late 1800s with higher levels of literacy, aided by new printing technology and an abundance of different types of writers. An astonishing era, like this 21st century phenomenon, the blog, linking the rise of the internet to new forms of exposition. Those early sequential stories were numbered, like chapters in a novel or movements in classical music, and called fascicles, meaning stories in parts. Also refers to any bundle of structures, like nerve or muscle fibers. A blog, like fascicles, threads thoughts and feelings together to share.

The next day, the student pointed out the flood of comments in response, all similar sentiment: *Blah, blah, blah. Have you seen him? Does he know how much you miss him?*

Admonished, she returned to form.

#44. Remember the first time you told me you loved me? We had known each other four weeks. We had lunch, we had dinner, we listened to music and watched movies, went to bed early and awakened at first light. I was giddy morning to night, atypical for a typically guarded woman. And then, one night, after a lecture at the library, we sat cattycorner to each other, our knees touching, at a hi-top table at a busy bar, and when the waitress put down our drinks, you raised your glass to mine and as we clinked, you said, here's to love, and then you leaned forward and said, what I mean is, I love you. I was speechless, although I already knew you were a romantic. I also knew you were impulsive – you had shared with me the rush to marry before and the challenge of staying married, once painfully aware of the mismatch. Impetuous versus pragmatic, perhaps the most pronounced of our temperamental differences. I sat back on my stool, astonished. You said I recoiled. I merely reverted to type. Tentative. Doubting. No one had ever captured my heart the way you had. I thought about you all day. I looked forward to your calls and messages. I felt the heat under my skin waiting to see you. Too much, too soon, too fast, for me. You're a sprinter, my love. I'm a pacer.

Subscribers cheered.

The next night, her mind churning with esoteric questions about what it means to be in love, she feverishly sketched notes for a more philosophical inquiry. If it's heat that attracts human beings, what binds us over time? Coupling, certainly marriage, historically, and until not long so ago, transactional. Still so in many lands. A financial or political alliance. A means to an end. Real love, happenstance. The accumulation of feeling. Alex used to say being in love was more important than loving. For him, passion was supreme, but for Angie, loving was the reward. Loving and yes, being loved. Romance is a spark; a fire requires a steady supply of fuel.

I've become a cliché, she moaned, even as the latest comments proved as weighty as academic discourse.

The editor invited her to lunch with her agent. She's over the moon about the blog. She proposes a book about the implosion, and fallout, of famous romantic relationships.

Stieglitz and O'Keeffe. Cleopatra and Ceasar. Henry and Eleanor of Aquitane. A treasure trove of material, she exclaims.

She suggests artwork they might adapt for the cover. Blurbs she will extract from well-known cultural commentators. She chats more effusively, and profusely, than she ever has, and then, as coffee is served, she leans toward Angie, places a hand on her arm and whispers, *You were brave to leave. Women are not always brave. So much easier to stay. I'm second to none in my adoration of Lennon and McCartney, but love is not all you need. Nietzsche, mad genius that he was, was on point when he said marriage based only on romantic love is on shaky ground. Quite right.*

She sits back in her chair and returns to business mode as abruptly as she morphed to confidante.

This book has stupendous potential, she proclaims. *Better than memoir or mindfulness, or even the nature of happiness, hot these days. This is the real deal. Speaks to everyone who has loved and lost, which is everyone.*

Flummoxed by the revealing personal response from someone seeming impervious, and again astonished by the nerve she seems to have inflamed, Angie abandoned the rest of the day's workload to blog.

#45. A friend said I was brave to leave. She admires what she thinks is courage. Yes, I was brave when I left a misguided marriage. Beyond that, I have never thought of myself as brave. Certainly not heroic. I hide cowardice. The people who know me best, know this. Do most women lack the courage to leave? Fear of loneliness, poverty, societal stigma? We have assimilated so fully the fairytale narrative of happily ever after, that we ignore, or dismiss, reality. The magnitude of unhappily married women suggests so. Men, as well, and, yes, this is a vast generalization, but research suggests men are more inclined to accessorize. Women, less likely to seek the comfort of lovers. We all want a warm bed. Speaking of beds, remember when we spent a weekend in Palm Springs? At the hotel, rolling around the king-size bed, I said it was such fun to have so much room we should upgrade at home from the queen to a king, and you replied, why would we want to be farther apart? You are the most intimate man I've ever known. I should not have let you go, despite my fear of being hostage to your intensity. Self-preservation is not the same as bravery. An essential distinction.

Spent from the verbal theatrics, Angie collapsed on the couch listening to NPR and then took a long evening walk on a path high in the hills, soothed by evening breezes and the canopy of leaves on tall trees. Walkers and runners passed, glued to their headphones, but couples strolled in sync, chatting, some hand in hand. Angie wondered what sort of struggles they face. What compromises they make. She watched a descendant sun spread shockwaves of color above the horizon. There are dramatic sunsets across the globe, she thought. Perhaps she will start over somewhere else.

She posted to Twitter…

I may be in need of a change of scene. Somewhere we have no footprints. Where I won't catch the scent of you. But how will I leave where you are? The place we were one?

That night, after a few hours of sleep, Angie awakened in thrall to an erotic dream. Her body convulsed with pleasure, as if caressed, and she laughed at a woman her age as horny as an adolescent. Disconnected from reason to rapture. She seized the moment for pleasure, and afterwards bundled into a robe, turned on soft music, lit a candle in the den, its wavy edges casting willowy shadows on the wall, and curled up on the sofa with a novel she's been meaning for ages to read. A delight she once enjoyed during middle of the night wakeups, but forfeited for Alex, because he groaned when she left the bed. He gifted her a book light to read there, but she was hesitant to disturb him. Of late, obsessed with bemoaning the loss of love, she has overlooked the pleasures of living alone, like reading on the sofa in the stillness of the wee hours. Although the novel was engaging, her eyelids grew heavy and she pulled a throw blanket over her to sleep there. In the morning shower, she missed Alex, but longed for him a little less.

A few hours later, as if a cosmic joke, eight weeks into the blog, five months after they parted, and just when Angie glimpsed light at the end of the tunnel, she ran into Alex.

She was on her way to pick up tea before class, and as she approached the café, Alex emerged. They both stopped in their tracks. He smiled. She smiled. He reached out his arms for her and she fell into his clutch of a hug, warm and lingering. When she said she was on her way to class, he offered to escort her. As they strolled, they chatted amiably, like old friends. She asked about his kids, his work, his back. She admired an Apple watch he wore.

A gift, he said, with a sheepish grin, and she knew her replacement gifted the watch.

She must like you a lot, she said.

Alex shrugged. *She has come and gone.*

There was an awkward silence between them as they awaited a light to cross to campus.

And what are you working on these days? Alex asked.

Believe it or not, a blog, she answered.

A blog? he replied. *Tell me, what makes a blog a blog? Not a short essay or an Op-ed? A client suggested I blog, but I don't see how it fits, for me.*

I'm still a novice. Lots of different blogs out there. Mostly, I think, it's about sharing experience or expertise. Point of view. Mark Twain would have been a good blogger. Jonathan Swift. George Orwell. I was told there should be a message, beyond a hook.

And what's your message?

Not sure I've nailed that down yet.

I'll read yours. Will be a good model.

Angie froze, panicked. If Alex reads the blog, will he appreciate the sentiment, or be infuriated by the disclosure? She's sure she never mentioned his name, but she should have used a pseudonym. Will he understand her intent, or take offense?

A waste of time, she protested. *Merely a writing exercise. Wouldn't interest you.*

Everything you do interests me.

And there, they ran out of words, and time. They hugged again, and Angie trembled at the nearness of him. His warmth. His scent. Abandoning restraint, she whispered into his ear, *I miss you, Alejandro.*

Although he was named Alexander, she called him Alejandro. The language of lovers. Something she would never disclose in a blog.

I'm sorry I wore you out, he whispered, and abruptly let go and walked away.

Later that day, Alex texted. *Nice to see you, Lina.* Short for Angelina, her full name. Sexier, he said, the first time they made love, and from then on, Lina and Alejandro.

She turned their encounter into a post.

#46. A close encounter of the third kind. Very close. A warm hug. The pleasure of your scent. Afterward, you sent a text saying nice to see me. Nice? Such a bland word. Great to see you, or happy to see you, would have meant more. That tender hug suggested you were pleased to see me, but your word, so passive. Unemotional. On the other hand, you used your pet name for me, a nickname that represents the best of me, and I was, in truth, at my best with you, until I wasn't. Maybe that's the summary statement. People in love should bring out the best in each other. I fear we did not. I'm so glad your life seems on an even keel, no longer the roller coaster ride we shared, but will you ever understand that everything that happened to you happened to me? You had me, but I was on my own. When I said I was worn out, I was genuinely worn out. I needed your strength, your kindness, even if unable to ask for it. Instead you moved out and moved on, outraged by my failure. In truth, we failed each other. Still, you seemed glad to see me, as I was to see you.

Late that night, sleepy and restless, a comment from one of her followers caught her eye. *Do you really miss him or are you lonely?*

She answered by weaving the historical into the essence of the blog.

#47. Consider Queen Elizabeth. The first Elizabeth. The redhead with a collar rising up around her neck like a brace, popularized on PBS and in film. Her long reign was stained by struggle for the throne and the partitioning of Catholic and Protestant, and, for years, a war torn country. She is also acknowledged for her patronage of the arts. Above all, Elizabeth's story is the so-called Virgin Queen. As a child she famously declared she would never marry, although there were many suitors. She longed for one man all her life. A childhood friend. Their devotion is legendary, platonic or sexual, never confirmed. When she ascended to the throne, age twenty-five, she named him Master of the Horse, an honored position that gave him free access to her in the palace. She trusted his loyalty. He was married by then, although there was speculation that during a period of time when she was bedridden with a so-called bloating illness, she was pregnant, and years later, a young man claimed to have been the love child whisked away. Never confirmed. Later in life, the widowed Dudley mounted a courtship in the hope of capturing his queen at last, but she resisted, fearing repercussions. Their friendship faltered. A sad story – bathed by attention from birth to death, Elizabeth was a lonely woman. She may have loved him. She signed her many letters, as you know, ever the same. Their relationship lasted fifty years. More than most marriages, certainly then. For me, solitude is tolerable, often essential, and yes, at times, I am lonely. Mostly I miss the man I love.

She tweeted the synopsis…

One can be a loner, one can learn to live

alone as an independent spirit, without being lonely. I am lonely only for the man I lost.

The next day, Angie receives a text from Alex. *Take down the blog.*

She takes a deep breath and texts back. *Let's talk.*

Nothing to talk about. People will know it's me. You used me. How could you?

That was never the intent.

Take down the blog.

Readers are strangers, they don't know you.

Take down the blog.

Did you read it all?

Take down the blog.

Please Alex, let's talk.

It's a monologue. Totally one-sided.

Please, let me explain, she texts.

First take down the blog.

I will, she replies, albeit hesitating a few seconds before she hits send. *When can we meet?*

Half an hour later, an excruciatingly slow ticking of the clock, Angie grows frantic, until Alex messages again. *Tell me where and when and I'll meet you there and then.*

She smiles. She'd forgotten the poetry in him. At the same moment, a follower sends a message. *Never give up on someone you can't go a day without thinking about.*

Angie ponders the message. Can lovers ever fully scrub the slate and start again?

She sits at the dining table taking notes on shifting the focus of the blog to second chances. She might examine famous liaisons, as the editor urged, with an eye on reformation. How many famous or infamous couples have split and returned to each other? How many have been successful? She has a following now. The agent will get her a good advance. She will have the time to research. Her student assistant has been urging her to charge a nominal fee for subscriptions. She might take sabbatical.

She's ecstatic at the prospect of such a juicy project. A chance to flex scholarly muscles differently. She never could have imagined all this and she cannot imagine giving it up.

She glances at the clock. She glances at the landing page of the blog. She will have to leave now or she will be late to meet Alex. She assumes he is already waiting at a hi-top table at the same bistro bar where he first told her he loved her, scanning his phone, glancing to the door now and then. Expectant. Hopeful.

How long will he wait?

Present Tense

The day was cool, brisk, the sun high and warming, and streets bustling with traffic, the financial district, timeworn, beleaguered, transformed seemingly overnight into a trendy place to live and work. Lyn imagined she must seem a tourist, perusing the last few smaller buildings, history embedded in cracked brick and blurred historic plaques, before peering up to the many new, impossibly tall and narrow, gleaming glass and steel skyscrapers, pointing ever higher to the sky. Lower Manhattan so dramatically changed, more now like Dubai.

Few pockets of nostalgia, mere shadows of past tense, too soon forgotten.

John had suggested they break bread, his words, at a popular bistro near his office. *If you don't mind,* he said. *Reliably good,* he added, as if she required persuading.

As she had recently resettled from her suburban home to an apartment a little more than a mile north, she decided to walk. Still her nerves. She had not, but should have expected to be uneasy at meeting him, the shock of his existence still acute, and as she approached the restaurant, the knot that had fastened into her gut when she first heard the news, twisted tighter. The word that came to mind in the shower this morning was spooky. Creepy, her younger grandson might say, like in a house of horrors, skeletons and demons popping eerily from the darkness.

Seriously, I can almost hear atonal music, a singular repeated note, or two, a cello, rising from the lower register, primal, like Jaws, threatening imminent doom, Lyn confessed to her daughter, Drew, when she called to check in, mimicking the sound in a deep drone.

You're being completely ridiculous, Drew spouted, laughing. *Really, he's a lovely man. I can vouch for him. You need to get over all this.*

Drew was the one who instigated *all this* a few months ago. Merely out of curiosity, she said, she submitted to one of those fashionable genetic analyses, hoping to unearth a more remarkable bloodline than just German Irish.

She could not have imagined the fallout: the Pandora's Box of the modern age.

Soon after she received the certification

of her lineage, which turned out to be purely German Irish, Drew received a notice her DNA matched closely with another client and, after agreeing to allow him to make contact, they met, online, as she lives in London, eight years now, with her British husband and son. Lyn visits, usually in the fall, last year at Christmas, the season in the city of Dickens a delight, and Drew and the family return summers to spend time with Lyn, and with friends in the area, before a holiday with sister Jen and her family on Cape Cod, a longstanding tradition.

They called it a match as close as a planet orbiting the sun. Rare, they said, Drew told Lyn, whom she called at once when she received the news. *A first-level relative, a sibling or parent,* she cried, as if she had excavated ancient treasure.

The son, they discovered, Lyn's late husband, Jerome, never knew he had.

Since Lyn had nothing whatsoever to do with this boy, a boy-man, she thinks of him, fathered when Jerome was still in college, long before they met, she had little interest in him, at first, and her girls were concerned she might be bothered by his existence.

Not at all. Makes no difference so long after the fact, she countered.

Her first thought, then and still, was that Jerome, who died ten years ago, would have liked to know he had a son.

He looks a little like dad, Drew reported to Lyn and Jen after her first video meeting with John. *In the eyes. The same soft blue. A little in the smile. Restrained, warm, like Dad's. He's a bit shy, well, no, reserved, would be the better word.*

Like Dad, Jen murmured, voice cloaked in melancholy.

The grief her daughters share, although less on the surface over time, is no less severe. Subcutaneous sorrow, forever present.

Jerome was nearing seventy, still robust, planning his retirement. *Up to the challenge,* he told them, proudly, until cancer proved too formidable a challenge.

Drew, a history professor, a Buddhist, her embrace of the journey as absolute as the historic timelines she adheres to, contends that her father's spirit manifests often as a wren or a robin in her garden. Jen, a child psychologist, harbors her sorrow like a baby bird in the nest.

A descendant, a junior version, in effect, incomprehensible.

He must feel strange, I mean, to be in such an unusual situation, Jen remarked. *But what will he get from knowing us? A health history?*

Lyn shares her younger daughter's caution, although she feels badly for the son. Must be awful to locate a biological father, only to realize he will never know him.

When Drew mentioned that John and his family lived for thirty years in a town on the eastern bank of the Hudson River, the same town where Lyn wanted to live when she and Jerome first moved out of the city, she had one of those unnerving time-warp sensations. The ground beneath her feet turned gelatinous, as if she might be sucked into a sink hole. Jerome suggested at the time they move inland to a small city with a historic town square and good schools, closer to his brothers and families, who lived in Connecticut. A good place to raise their daughters. She wonders now, if they had settled in the smaller town, would they have shopped at the same stores? Dined at the same restaurants? If their paths had crossed, would they have felt drawn to each other, as if a metaphysical connection?

I think you'd both like him, Drew pressed, by way of reassurance. *One of those likeable guys, like Dad.*

Jerome, a man renowned for affability.

Such a good guy, friends and colleagues echoed at the funeral. *Only the good die young,* Lyn responded, then and since.

Do you think he knew? Jen questioned.

No way, Drew retorted. *He could not have known. He would have stepped up, right?*

The question was meant for her mother.

Absolutely. If your father had known he had another child, he would have wanted to know him. He would have offered financial support. He would have told me.

He would have liked to have a son, Jen said.

He loved his girls, Lyn replied, gently reproaching.

But my sister is named Drew because he wanted a boy, Jen argued.

Family lore.

We picked the name to be gender neutral, you know that, Lyn said. *He adored his girls, he was proud to be your father.*

In truth, she was not obligated to affirm Jerome's affection. No need to defend him. The departed, particularly those who die too soon, canonized – faults forgiven, failures dismissed. The surviving parent the remaining bearing wall and repository of lingering discontent.

Dad was what, forty-two when I was born?

Drew chimed in. *He complained he was old, but he never seemed old, right Jen? Did what he would have done with a son – shot hoops with us. Kicked the soccer ball around. Taught us to play poker.*

He preferred playing board games, or taking us to the zoo, Jen reminisced.

He may have liked to have a son, don't all men? But he was happy with us, Drew insisted.

Exactly right, Lyn declared.

Jen clung to her caution, more troubled by the secret revealed than the fact, never one to encourage or embrace change, although she facilitates just that for her clients.

Drew leapt into the delight of claiming a big brother, she the one to relish each and all manifestations of destiny.

A half-brother, Jen reminded her when she referred to him as her brother.

Okay, fine, but we gelled, Jen. Really, you would like him, she said.

What did you talk about? Lyn asked.

I filled in a few details, you know, where we grew up. How we used to play marathon Monopoly games on Sunday. The way Dad mucked up carving the Thanksgiving turkey, every time. That stuff.

At the holiday memory, they laughed.

What does he do? Jen inquired.

Financial analyst, Wall Street, Drew said.

He and dad would have spoken the same language, Jen grumbled.

That her father was often preoccupied with business bothered her since childhood. The long hours he kept. The stress she believed killed him.

Did you save any of dad's ledgers, Mom? He might like to see them, Drew asked, ignoring her sister's grousing.

Lyn paused to consider, brow furrowed as if the effort alone restores memory. *In one of the boxes in storage, I'm pretty sure.*

Only recently, downsizing, she cleared out the last of Jerome's belongings, a few select memorabilia packed for her daughters in bins labeled *Dad*. Yes, she saved a few of the many ledgers climbing like ivy on shelves behind his desk. All the same size and binding, quadrille lined, where he kept track of banking, vacation expenses, car and mortgage payments, capital expenditures, and such. Famous for precision, he refused to use spreadsheets, preferring the grip of a pencil in hand. The scratch on paper.

He has a daughter. I saw her picture. Close to your age, Jen, Drew said.

Our father's son has a daughter my age?

Trace the timeline. Dad would have been eighty this year. John is sixty. His daughter is thirty-two, Drew expounded, lapsing into a professorial tone of voice.

Does she look like him? Lyn chimed in.

A little, Drew answered. *A little like Jen.*

I'm sorry, but the weird is getting weirder, Jen muttered.

Will take getting used to, yes, Lyn agreed.

I still wonder what he wants, Jen mused.

He's interested in who he is, in an existential way. I would have thought you would understand the psychology, Drew badgered her sister.

It's because I understand the psychology I am questioning his motives, Jen retorted. *We are not responsible for filling in his blanks. Boundaries must be maintained.*

Where is your kindness? Drew snapped.

You could show me a little kindness, Jen cried. *Maybe I need more time to process.*

If he wants to learn more about Jerome, I would be happy to chat with him, Lyn interceded, surprising both. *Not that I have anything to do with this, long before my time, but I knew your father well. The man, beyond the dad. If John wants to know Jerome from a broader perspective, tell him he's welcome to contact me.*

She had not imagined the sound of his voice would bring her husband back from the grave. When he called, when he first said hello, she gasped, his voice as deep, as sonorous as Jerome's, who spoke with the modulation of an audio book narrator. From the first, beyond his hypnotic eyes, the gentle smile, it was the cadence of his voice that warmed her heart.

She kept his message on their home voice mail for years, until she gave up the land line. Cutting the cord, not the longing.

I've been looking forward to meeting you, so to speak, John said, *although, frankly, I've been anxious about it.*

The sort of thing his father would never have divulged, allowing most water to run off his back, absorbing, perhaps, a few droplets. What a DNA test will not reveal.

Well, this is a most unusual situation, isn't it? Lyn answered.

Indeed. I suppose Drew filled you in.

Some. Quite a revelation, so late in life. How are you handling all this?

She had to suppress a laugh at herself, slipping instantly into maternal mode. A voice she once adopted with her daughters to calm their nerves before a school play or sports.

Frankly, I'm not sure I'm glad Mom told me, he said. *Maybe ignorance is bliss.*

She must have had her reasons.

She was very young at the time.

A terribly difficult decision, Lyn agreed.

What the women of her generation dealt with. Options few. Shame assimilated.

I get that, John said. *I do. On the other hand, my stepfather was not a good man.*

He spoke matter-of-factly, as if merely describing a character in a film, although she detected the hurt in his voice.

And how nice it might have been to have sisters. Also cousins to my daughter, he added.

How is she handling this?

She's as enthusiastic as Drew. They will get on well. However, today's women, they don't fully comprehend what women then had to deal with. How this sort of thing played out.

Tell me how it happened, Lyn encouraged, curious, and, in the moment, wanting to bond with her husband's son.

So John told her the story, as if the telling would help make sense of it.

The summer between junior and senior years at a small college upstate, Jerome worked on a construction site roughly one hundred miles up-river. When he told Lyn about it, he said he'd never been as exhausted at the end of the day. Also, superhuman strength, beyond anything he felt before or since, he crowed. At the end of their 10-hour shift, the crew stopped at a local dive for a beer and a burger, before collapsing onto cots set up in a temporary shelter near the site. John's mother was the one waitress. A high school graduate, a statuesque blonde with blue eyes and a bright smile, she was the quintessential all-American girl of that era. Jerome was different from the local boys who gaped and groped. The college boy, she called him, and with him, she discovered erotic pleasure laced with a tenderness she had not yet experienced. After his workday, he napped until her shift ended, and they slept together at her studio above a shop down the street. Sundays, they lingered in bed late into the morning until, depleted, famished, they fled to a diner for a hearty breakfast. They took long walks along a creek bed and swam in a lake. He read to her the business news – mergers and acquisitions, stock market yields and ratios – thoughtfully explaining the terms. She was stunned by his appetite – for food, for learning, and for her. By summer's end, she knew she was pregnant, and she knew Jerome would do the right thing.

She also knew she wasn't ready to settle down, she told John, when she confessed.

In those days, she explained, from her hospice bed, *girls were taught to secure a man to take care of us, and for him to be taken care of in return. However, we were nothing alike. He was ambitious. Planning to pursue an MBA. Said he would be a CEO someday, in New York City. The place to be, he said. Not for me. I'm a country girl. It was a summer fling, that's all. Not meant to be forever. I knew I had to let go.*

Your mom was incredibly self-aware for one so young, Lyn observed. *I'm not sure I would have had the presence of mind, not then.*

My mom was also not one to make waves, John replied. *She confided to the priest. He said she would be forgiven. And when he interceded with her parents, she was banished to one of those unwed mother warehouses.*

All too common then.

Yes, but when she refused to give me up for adoption, her parents withdrew their support.

She moved farther upstate and tapped a neighbor to stay with John at night, while she waitressed. She was pursued by a lumberman, a solid citizen, she thought. She told him her husband died of pneumonia. She claimed she was an orphan.

He must have liked the idea of being her savior. A fixer, he was, also fixated on a very rigid view of right and wrong, John said.

They married and moved into a house in the woods. Like a fairy tale, she believed, her past fully swept under a new rug.

He took responsibility her, and for me, I'll give him that, although not the happily ever after my mother hoped for.

What was her name? Lyn asked, needing to brand the romance Jerome never revealed.

Jane, John answered, and laughed. *Such a plain name, but never a plain Jane.*

She did what was best, for you and for her.

Sure, but my adoptive father was a tyrant. And then, when I was three, they had another son, and he lost all interest in me. I went from first to last, to nothing, in truth, overnight, and it only got worse over the years.

Why? I hope you don't mind me asking, Lyn questioned.

You can ask me anything, but the truth is, I never understood beyond the status of siblings, you know, one or the other favored. Now that I know the truth, I realize I was a reminder of the other man in my mother's bed. My stepfather convinced himself of the nobility of his commitment, but he was not noble. It's that simple. I get it now. A little late, but better than not, I suppose.

She should have intervened, in some way, Lyn thought. She should have protected her son from feeling worthless.

Jerome would have liked to have a son and I'm happy to tell you more about him, so you might know him, Lyn said.

They agreed to meet for a late lunch at a café downtown. He was waiting for her out front, at the signpost, standing erect, alert, like a doorman. Lyn recognized him at once by his stance: sturdy, broad shouldered, not as tall as Jerome, but similarly commanding. She stared at him. Jerome's son. He loved his daughters and appreciated the friendship and admiration of many women, but he was a man's man. He played three sports in high school and two in college. He played pickup basketball in town for years, then switched to golf when his knees refused to bounce. Lyn was certain that if he'd known he'd had a son, he would have made it a point to spend time with him. Toss a ball, watch football, play cards. The way men bond.

She stared at him through a third light change, before crossing the street. As she drew near, he perked up, as if he knew her, and reached out his hands for hers. Her daughter, she realized, must have shared photos.

They held the shake a little longer than strangers do. More like fond acquaintances. What are we? Lyn wondered. Just ten years between them. Not old enough to be his mother or a stepmother. An aunt, perhaps? Or, they might be friends. Of course, they will be friends, she decided.

The café, in the shadow of the Freedom Tower, not far from the 9/11 memorial, had been carved out of a century old storehouse and remodeled in the modern industrial style: triple story ceilings, exposed wood beams and aluminum ductwork, original cement floors polished, their cracks and scars preserved for authenticity. Metal chairs were cushioned in maroon, like late autumn leaves before they brown. A massive iron chandelier with electric candles lit the entry and the blades of a broad ceiling fan rotated hypnotically above a seating area illuminated by skylights.

The juxtaposition of past and present setting the scene, Lyn thought.

Everything old is new again, John said, as they sat, as if reading her mind.

I like a place with a vibe, she answered.

He smiled, noticeably relieved. Just like his father, she thought, who always wanted to make things right for everyone else.

I have a fondness for the historic, she said. *I mean, places that hold history, even if not ancient, like this. Old houses restored, not remodeled.*

She was rambling, the sign of anxiety. She took a deep breath to calm down.

The old and the new interactive, so to speak, he commented.

So to speak, she replied, feeling foolish nattering on about architecture in the first moments of a momentous meeting.

I once wanted to be an architect, and I would absolutely have merged old with new, John said.

What stopped you?

Life. Life gets in the way. I'm good with numbers. I'm not inventive, I lean to the concrete, he said, with a shrug, pointing to the floor.

Jerome was the same, she said.

He smiled, pleased at the comparison.

An awkward moment of silence ensued and Lyn wondered now if Drew had convinced him to meet her. He might have felt obliged.

I'm not sure where to start, he remarked. *I'm honestly not sure what I want to know or even how much more I want to know.*

Let's get the food thing out of the way first, she said, to which he nodded, relieved.

She scrutinized him over the rim of the menu. Not a replica of Jerome, but undeniably similar. The deep-set blue eyes, but closer knit. The Romanesque nose, slightly wider at the tip. Oval face, more elongated. The lips, however, on closer notice, exactly the same – modest in size and shape, and the lower lip pleasingly plump, the shade of a ripe apple.

Lips meant to kiss. Meant to enfold the delicate parts of a woman's body.

She quivered.

Are you cold? Want to move? he asked.

No, no, I'm fine. Maybe I'll order tea.

He smiled. *Good idea. And, well, tell me, please, if you need anything you don't have.*

If she told him the many things she no longer has, or what she needs, she would seem a sad old widow, exactly how she would rather not be perceived.

Sorry to have made you lunch so late, I bet you're hungry, he said.

I'm always hungry, she replied. *That's not*

to say I eat whenever or whatever I want, but I have a good appetite for good food.

She ordered beet salad with goat cheese and he, a tuna melt on rye.

Yes, he responded to the waiter's query about fries, beseeching Lyn to share. *Save me!*

She laughed. *Happy to help you out.*

When the tea arrived, as she squeezed lemon into the brew, her eyes lowered, she was aware of him observing her, as curious about her as she him. Perhaps he too wondered what sort of bond they might forge.

She looked up to meet his gaze. *You must feel a little like a stranger in a strange land.*

That sums it up quite well, although your daughter has been a wonderful guide.

She nodded. *She's happy to know you.*

The same, he replied. *But Jen, maybe not.*

Jen takes her time. She'll come around. She has a tender heart.

I'm sure.

So, I have to ask, and I'm sorry to sound like a prosecutor, but, well, I get why your mother didn't make it known right away, but why not sooner?

I appreciate your directness. I have no time, nor further use for veils.

Is that what it was, why your mother never

told you who your father was? Was she always, as you suggest, veiled?

Deceptive is the word you're not saying, and yes, she was, although I believe it was a response to a repressed childhood, and then, by nineteen, tossed out on her own. When she let down, which she did with us, my brother and I, she was all there. I think we lightened her load.

Of course you did. Maybe she was afraid to lose your respect, Lyn pondered aloud.

He nodded. *Hard to make sense of your life when your dying mother says you're not who you think you are. Your heritage, identity, altogether different from all you'd been led to believe.*

Why do you think she told you in the end?

I asked. What I mean is, I asked if there was anything she wanted me to know. Last chance to set me straight, Mom, I said, expecting maternal pearls of wisdom. Maybe a memory she cherished. There's so much we fail to ask in real time, and with my mother, little was forthcoming without probing.

You sure got more than you were expecting.

Even more than you know, he said, with an expression like Jerome's when confounded by hateful or nonsensical human behavior.

Lyn waited him out.

I haven't mentioned this to Drew. But, well,

you might as well know, Mom also confessed that my brother's father was also not my adoptive father. Apparently my mother sought comfort with other men. She never told my brother either.

She was unhappy. She didn't want you to judge her poorly. I'm surprised she told you at all.

I was as well. I'd rather not have known.

Has your brother contacted his birth father?

He has no interest. Just biology, he said. He doesn't have the same curiosity. Or is it just my need for precision?

She chuckled. *Are you glad now, to know what you know?*

I'm glad to know you, he replied, with a warm smile.

Jerome's smile. A smile that alights first in the eyes, then glides to the lips, as if a kiss. A smile that makes a woman feel essential.

In that moment, in his smile, the young Jerome, the love of her life, emerged, returned to her, vigorous and as seductive as he was nearly to the end. An electric charge surged through Lyn's body. She felt her heart pound, as it had the first time Jerome touched her skin. The first time they made love, and the last.

Jerome favored the same aftershave all his life. A distinctive scent, woodsy, masculine, a little sweet, like sap from an ancient tree. Every time her cheek brushed against his, every time they kissed, intoxicating. After he died, she took the last bottle from the medicine cabinet and trickled a droplet on her pillow, every night, until emptied to melancholy.

Nietzsche referred to marriage as a very long conversation, and their conversation was not yet complete when, seven months after the diagnosis, Jerome was gone. Revived now in his son, perhaps to resume the dialogue.

She had a sudden chilling and thrilling thought: they could be lovers. Stranger things have happened. She took a deep breath to slow her hurried heartbeat. Calm the sexual current. Jerome's son, not Jerome, she scolded herself.

John was watching her, attentively. She could not imagine his thoughts, although she sensed an attraction. Or was it merely the need to connect? Bonded by circumstance.

Get a grip, she told herself.

What else would you like to know about Jerome? I mean, what would you like to know you have yet to learn from Drew? she asked, shifting the focus back to the father from the son.

Okay, well, would he have liked this place? A place with a vibe?

He preferred what he called decorum. Cloth tablecloths, a din more than a buzz. Not Michelin star places, not high end, and hardly epicure, just a bit more formal.

Got it, he said.

What else?

Well, tell me more about how he spent his days. What sort of husband he was. Knowing you will connect me to him, at a deeper level, I mean, if that's not too much of an imposition.

She shook her head no, but where to start? She could tell him they had disparate taste in more than restaurants. She wanted to live in the city, he to work here, but reside in the rustic. Their politics were often in conflict, he the more conservative. She had little interest in sports, certainly not weekend television marathons. She has an Irish temper, and he, a German passive-aggression. Still, they could never have imagined being apart and days before his end, they reaffirmed their vows, toasting with apple juice in champagne flutes.

She thought she knew everything there was to know about him.

Lyn can describe every last detail in the hospice room the night Jerome took his last breath. Beeping machinery. The sterile scent.

Late day rays of light through window blinds lining stripes on the tile floor. The sound of Jerome's steady, shallower breathing, until the death rattle. One final shudder. And then, the nudge of a nurse prying her from his bedside. She could not, however, describe, then or now, what she felt – emotion suspended in favor of the desire to remain alert to him, and for him, and then, once he was gone, she felt nothing. Hollow, parched, like a creek bed in drought.

In this moment, in the café with John, she was conscious only of him, the periphery faded to gray, as if a noir film. She heard no sound, felt nothing but the vibrations of her body. Longing unleashed from past to present.

Is it possible to reclaim what's been lost?

You're divorced, I understand, she said, still trying to perpetuate normal conversation.

Several years. I wasn't a good husband. Self-absorbed. Always trying to prove myself...

To your stepfather?

To myself, I suppose, like all of us, in the end.

But you were a good father, Lyn stated.

I appreciate your presumption. I do my best. I adore my daughter.

Lunch was served and they laughed at a basket piled high with crispy brown potatoes.

Gripped by feelings as bewildering as invigorating, Lyn picked at her salad. Nibbled a few fries. Sipped the tea.

Is the food all right? John inquired.

He would take it as his responsibility if not, like his father.

Yes. I guess I wasn't as hungry as I thought.

Take your time, he said.

She ate another fry. *Yum,* she feigned.

He laughed, and she laughed with him.

On her first date with Jerome, they shared a hamburger at a neighborhood bistro. Juices dripped to their chins. Ketchup oozed off shoestring fries. He had a beer, she a diet coke, and then, once sated, so she thought, he called for the dessert menu.

Let's splurge, he said, with that smile she would rarely dispute.

They agreed on apple cobbler, browned and bubbly, redolent of cinnamon, a scoop of vanilla ice cream melting into cream along the edges. Neither noticed when the waiter place two spoons on the table for them, mesmerized by each other. As she is drawn now to his son.

When my daughters were young, she said, *I used to ask them to describe their dreams and I wrote them down. The dream journals, we called them. They do the same now, with their children. Morning minds so fertile. Uninscribed. Hard to remember once past tense. So, do you recall any of your dreams then? The real or the imagined?*

She heard in her voice the maternal, but also a flirtatious note, and she hoped he hadn't noticed. He considered his response, briefly, before leaning forward into their tête à tête, their eyes locked.

I rarely remember dreams, but I remember a sort of dream-state on my bike on the ride home from school. I moved slowly, always happier out of the house, and most days, before I had an afternoon job, I'd take a loop around the neighborhood, and end up feted by the other moms with fresh cookies. I was a skinny kid. They must have thought I was starving. So, a dream scenario, of a sort.

Starving for affection, Lyn imagined. *Your father had a penchant for sweets. What else? What pleases you, besides fries?*

He laughed.

I am pleased to know my biological family. Otherwise, well, I don't spend much time thinking about what pleases me, or what I'm sorry for either, maybe like my mother that way.

You don't have to confess anything to me.

I would not be inclined to confess anything

*to a stranger, but you're hardly a stranger, I mean,
not anymore,* he said, with a grateful smile.

Do you still ride a bike?

He laughed. *Hardly. Not for a long time.
And no one offers me warm cookies.*

She laughed, loudly, elatedly, delighted
by the sound of her laughter, the sheer ecstasy
of being so near Jerome's life force. She had to
restrain a desire to reach out and take his hand.

Your turn, he entreated.

*I rarely remember sleep dreams, but I've had
childhood dreams come true, like, for some reason,
the one leaping to mind is my first trip out of the
country. After college graduation, a bare bones
holiday with girlfriends, across France. I drove a
standard shift car, first time. A blue Citroen with
faded leather seats that smelled of the sun.*

She remembers being enthralled by the
sultry language, the landscape, new foods and
ancient faces. She had toyed with the idea of
moving there, to a town where lavender blows
in the breeze, but she had a job to return to. A
man she looked forward to loving. She used to
berate Jerome for taking so long.

What an odd juxtaposition, she thought:
wife and son, longing for the same man.

She trembled again and John reached

out his hand to cover hers. A touch of comfort, which nonetheless exacerbated the trembling. She sat very still, breathing slowly to sublimate the arousal.

I'm fine, I tend to cold, she said.

Cold hands, warm heart, he said, his eyes on hers, even as he withdrew his hand, as if he, too, startled by desire.

Your father wasn't as… she stumbled, reaching for the right words.

Wasn't what? he asked.

Not as aware a person as you seem to be, nor as inquisitive. Intellectually, yes, but he was more often focused on what he wanted to accomplish. A purpose-driven man, highly productive.

I wish I took after him that way. I tend to procrastinate. My daughter calls it waffling.

We have that in common, Lyn said.

Contradictions in character define a person, more than the predictable, would you agree?

Absolutely. Who wants to be predictable? she said, although she fears she is painfully so. *On the other hand, predictability is reliability. Your father was a man I could count on.*

So am I, he said, and then he blushed.

Oh, the charm of a man who blushes.

She rambled on, filling him in on family

lore, still hoping to defuse sexual chemistry, no matter how glorious the feeling. He nibbled on his sandwich, hanging on every word she said. She described Jerome's insistence on reserving, every summer, the same cottage on Cape Cod, for the family holiday. His frustration with the rapid advance of technology, concerns about invasions of privacy, and the predictions for AI. Loud swearing at TV sports, the only time he cursed. An eccentric preference for shoes without laces, and, at home, slippers.

He hated to be barefoot, except on the sand, she remarked.

Why was that?

You know, I don't know. Some things just are as they are, Lyn replied, thinking, yes, there were some things she didn't know about him, but none that matter.

What music did he like? John asked.

Everything but country, and even a little country, the bluesy sort, she replied.

Right. My mother said he liked Bach and the Beatles, while she loved Tammy Wynette. Like a partially frozen river, she said. Cannot be crossed.

Your mother was very expressive.

That she was.

And your stepfather liked country?

Yeah, but Johnny Cash country. A different sort of river, if you know what I mean.

I think I do.

The sky had turned gray beyond the skylights. A busboy cleared their plates and the waiter returned. They both declined his offer of coffee or dessert.

We've only just scratched the surface, John murmured.

She glanced at her watch to discover it was nearly evening. The lonely hours. Worse in autumn, the days shorter, too soon dark.

I imagine you have to get back to work, or catch a train? she said.

No. No commitments. And you?

Well, I'm footloose and fancy free, as they say. The retired life has its pleasures.

I look forward to it.

Jerome and I often enjoyed an after-dinner drink, when we were traveling.

Nice. What was his drink of choice?

Kahlua, or a Brandy. I think he liked the hold of snifters, the clink of the ice, more than the drink.

And you?

Amoretto. I prefer a nutty flavor.

So let's find a classy bar. The new hotels here are hip, he suggested, with an enticing smile.

Passion subsumed reason. The lure of an indiscretion irresistible, albeit irrational. She seemed unable to restrain her emotions, even knowing she might be going too far.

You know, I live just a long walk from here, although… She hesitated. Having a drink at her apartment might invite reckless behavior. A liaison for which neither was prepared. Her daughters would be appalled. She's appalled at herself, although captive to the fantasy.

We have so much more to share, he said, as if to neutralize her hesitance. He took her hand. *The truth is, I could be with you hours and hours, days and months and years,* he crooned.

At these words, Lyn startled. *Sorry, what was that you said?*

Just a saying, from long ago.

I could be with you hours and hours, days, and months and years, she recited.

Yes, that's it.

Unusual turn of phrase. Who said that?

He shrugged. *From a poem, I guess.*

Lyn flinched and pulled her hand away, recoiling, as if punched, against her chair.

The poetic expression your late father used to say! she reprimanded.

The sentiment, the exact words, Jerome

recited to the girls when he left on a trip or, apologetically, showed up late to an event.

I could be with you hours and hours, days and months and years.

The last words Lyn whispered to him.

John stared at her, revealed, remorseful.

So he did know! Lyn cried. *And you knew him? You spent time with him?*

I didn't know he was my father. I swear. My mother said he was a family friend. He came to visit, once a year, on my birthday, I think starting when I was a toddler. Maybe when my brother was born. She must have wanted an alternate male presence for me, even if only now and then.

When? When did he come?

June. June second. He gave me a suitcase, my first, for a summer trip to the Grand Canyon. Had the lock set to 0602, so I would never forget.

She nodded. He did the same for each of the girls with their first luggage.

Early June, she repeated, trying to recall where he was, rather where he said he was.

Fishing, upstate, with college buddies, every year, she remembers. He brought home trout packed in ice. So he made a detour on the way to see his son. As stealthy as a secret agent.

Why keep the secret? she cried.

Honestly, Lyn, he's as much a mystery to me as if I'd never known him at all. He disappeared, 38 years ago. Sent a graduation gift, but I never saw him again.

When Drew was born, she muttered.

Yes, I get that now.

Why wouldn't your mother tell you then?

I think she was afraid my adoptive father would find out. He had a terrible temper.

And you never noticed the resemblance?

You don't think you look like someone so much older, someone you hardly know, rarely see.

She pondered his words as fury filled her heart – at herself, at John, and, especially, at Jerome.

Deception, that's all this was. Your mother, my husband, and now you. Why didn't you tell us the truth? Why did you let us think you never knew him? What was the point of that?

I'm sorry. I'm so sorry. I, I didn't know what to expect when I went looking for you all. I wanted to learn about him as a father. I wanted to know his children. To know his wife. I knew at once the girls were in the dark, but I wasn't sure if you knew, and then, well, I guess I felt protective of him. I didn't mean to give him away. He had his reasons, I'm sure. He is, was, a good guy. He was kind to me.

A good guy. Her great love, the father of her children, a keeper of secrets, as it turns out. What else might he have kept from her?

Lyn, please, we can make this right. Let's keep talking. Let's have that drink, he implored.

The light in Lyn's eyes had turned dark. The reproach in her voice, severe. Neither the dead nor the living what they seemed.

You should have been straight with us from the start. We welcomed you. You might have had a relationship with the girls. An honest relationship. I would think that would matter to you after all this.

Yes, but…

You might have had a relationship with me!

We still can. The girls don't have to know.

She sighed and shook her head, sadly.

Have you learned nothing? Secrets wound. Secrets will out in the end.

Please, let's just walk, and talk, he pleaded.

I don't spend time with liars, she growled, and he hung his head in shame. *This would be so awful for the girls. They trusted their father. They believed him to be an honest man, as I did. None of this should have happened. Duplicity is never the right choice. You've upset a family apple cart.*

She stood abruptly, desperate to escape, nearly toppling her chair behind her, grasping at the back to steady herself as well.

I have to go, she cried, wobbly with rage, having fallen prey to deceit from her husband and his son, and ashamed of her foolish desire, mortified she might have surrendered to the delusion of turning back the clock.

Her heart ached, as if she were losing Jerome all over again.

John stood, watching her, helplessly, as she gathered her coat and bag.

I guess you are your father's son after all, she snarled, scowling still. *Your mother's as well. A veil, you said. A storybook word. The word is deceit. You cannot hide from this, not with us. I will not let you snare my daughters in your web.*

As she glared at him, she saw the tears in his eyes, and, with a deep relenting sigh, surprising them both, she stepped toward him to wrap her arms around his shoulders.

A maternal hug for her husband's son.

Breaking Hearts

Heaven is New York City, Lil mused, her dark eyes fixed on the cards in her hand, as if a mystery to be solved, shuffling with a customary sense of urgency – clustering suits, scanning digits, searching for the magic hand. *Especially on a lovely autumn afternoon. Oh those golden and red leaves,* she intoned, shaking her head side to side in that way women do when melancholy kicks in.

It's not quite fall, Edith remarked, crystal blue eyes squinting at her cards, the magnifiers hanging from a gold chain, like a pendant.

Heaven is Hawaii, Vera pronounced, as if gospel.

Vera's eyes too were glued to her cards, short bony fingers snapping one after another, front to back, and back again, until she landed on an optimum placement with a satisfied nod, like a sculptor, standing back to admire the finished work.

I'm still sad about Maui, Jeanette said.

Great holiday there, when the kids were small. We kayaked to where the green turtles breed. Hope the recovery goes well.

Are you planning to go back? Vera asked.

No, not possible, Jeannette replied. *Just… a fond memory.*

The others nodded their understanding, like parishioners at Sunday service.

Maybe someday, Edith soothed, patting Jeanette's hand. *You know, you girls are peasants. New York, Hawaii. For tourists,* she retorted, but with a chuckle.

Oh, excuse me, Lil snickered.

Excuse me, please, are you payin attention? Vera challenged Lil, who had laid down her cards to knead her neck, bangled wrist tinkling with each press of her fingers.

I most certainly am paying attention. What is your problem? Lil snarled.

You sure you want to discard that queen? Vera retorted.

Yes, I do.

You sure?

Yes, I am sure! Lil thundered.

Her companions turned to stare at her in consternation. Too early in the evening for Lil to turn ornery. She usually needs a couple of drinks to begin her lament, what her friends refer to, fondly, as nostalgia hour.

The four sat momentarily in silence, in their places, always the same configuration, on folding chairs matching the square wood table with brown and gold leather inlay. Vera never seats them at the dining table, an Ethan Allen relic she acquired when she married, fifty years ago, the wood as pristine and unmarred as the day it was delivered. *A dining table is for dining and a card table is a card table*, she insists.

These four old friends are the queens of the deck – spade and club, diamond and heart, their faces creased by age, and Southern sun, their bond, irrevocable, whatever quarrels or quibbles.

Seizing the moment, Lil repeated, *New York is the center of the universe, in every way, and what else might heaven be?*

My Lord, Jeanette muttered.

My Lord indeed! Edith bellowed, turning her cards face down on the table to run her long fingers through nearly fluorescent red curls. *My dear girl, Heaven is surreal. Not a place, not a destination, a realm. The closest thing on this earth may be a cornfield in Iowa blowing in the breeze. Or a vineyard in France at harvest. A mountaintop in*

Tibet, those monks think so. Or maybe that lake in the middle of that national park, you know the one I mean? We took the kids there one summer. Simply stunning. What's the name of that lake Jeanette, you remember don't you? I sent you a post-card.

You've sent me lots of post-cards, when was that one? Jeanette asked, with a smirk, the sort of expression reserved for a sibling.

Must be, let's see, Jesse just started middle school, Melinda was, yes, a freshman. My God she was surly that summer, Edith answered.

Darlin, that was, what, thirty years ago, or more? You think I remember every post-card you sent me from all your summer vacations? Jeanette said, and they all laughed, laughter contagious and curative, rippling around the table like the evening breeze wafting through lace curtains.

Jeanette shook her head, marveling at the incongruity of memory. Not everything can or needs remembering, she might have said, although her recall is unusually sound. A steel trap, Edith says, referring to her sister often for context and detail.

The irony, the offense, they all know, of Jeanette's husband, who has lost his recall for anything more recent than decades ago, so she serves as memory for him now as well.

From a distance, Jeanette might be taken for a younger woman. She has defied the worst ravages of age. Long and lean, thick ash blonde locks press against the nape of a graceful neck – she shares her sister's view that gray hair is an affront to femininity – and her makeup is, as always, expertly applied, enhancing porcelain skin she protects with a broad brimmed hat, the few wrinkles like feathered brush strokes.

And where is your version of heaven, Jeanette? Vera asked.

It sure is not this hand, Jeanette replied, laying her cards face down and smoothing the condensation on her beer bottle with a thumb. A marquis diamond engagement ring, nested into a studded platinum band, glistened in the light of the chandelier, the wedding ring she thinks of now as a prize for endurance.

The four play a while, sporadic silences punctuating their conversations like chapter breaks in a book. They commune well without words, intuiting each other's feelings by the rhythm of their breathing, their posture, how deep the furrows in their brows, and the ferocity of the shuffling of cards.

Frequent phone talks, evening walks, Sunday dinners with their families, and such, have woven these women together like cotton, and, for a decade, a weekly game of Hearts, not elegant, like Bridge, more like a blueprint for living: seek the right match, avoid missteps, protect the heart, and shoot, now and then, for the moon.

Jeanette licked a bit of foam at the rim of the bottle with a sigh of satisfaction and, as if a signal, the others paused to sip their drinks of choice. Edith favors white wine, Lil, gin and tonic, and Vera switches to sweet tea after the one glass of red wine she allows herself, the tea iced and poured from a crystal decanter on the sideboard, as if an aged liqueur.

Edith flicked a card and picked another, scanning it briefly before placing it where she felt it best belonged. Jeanette, waiting her turn, glanced through the latest edition of *Southern Living*, as Vera studied her cards, lips pursed, brow creased, she, the most studious among them. Lil, anxious to unload the perilous queen of spades, studied the cards on the table, while stretching one hand out, then folding back in, knuckles so swollen she no longer wears rings. She slapped her cards down to rub her neck.

Want a Motrin? Vera asked.

Not yet. That stuff flows through my veins

as it is. Another G&T will do fine, thank you.

Ever the perfect host, Vera stood, took Lil's glass and sailed into the kitchen, returning with a refill. Lil nodded her thanks and before returning to her seat, Vera scanned the table, then pulled a bottle of white wine from a bucket filled with ice, also on the sideboard, to refill Edith's glass, and grabbed a fresh bottle of beer for Jeannette, dropping the used, as if in slow motion, to minimize the clang, into a pail on the floor for discards.

I wish I were in New York right now, Lil mumbled wistfully, tired eyes radiating from mostly smooth, espresso skin, a bold dot of pink blush on her cheeks, like a Russian doll.

When I think of New York, I picture snow, Edith said, eyes on her cards. *I hate snow.*

Jeannette smiled, without comment. Since childhood, Edith has served as her shield, the elder sister more defiant, which proved a great advantage as Edith climbed a corporate ladder from secretary to the administrative director at a military supply firm, the first woman to rise to management. When Jeannette rails about what doesn't work as it should, the lack of courtesy in the service sector or the unfairness of the hand she's been dealt in recent years, she leans on her big sister for validation and, when stymied by cruelty, Edith steps up in her defense.

You know, I think I've only seen snow once or twice in my whole life, can you imagine? Vera said, smiling through molten brown eyes that seem to spring from her mocha skin.

Snow is majestic in the city, least it used to be, Lil said.

Of course it is, Edith said, rolling her eyes toward Jeanette.

But now, it's Indian summer up North, Lil remarked, sentimentality soaking her voice.

Yeah, hot and muggy, Edith sneered.

Sultry. Sexy and sultry is New York City in September, Lil crooned.

Damn, Lil, Jeannette barked, pounding her cards on the table and reaching for her beer. The others gaped at her with astonishment, as if she had just awakened from a coma. *Must we forever listen to you moaning over your lost youth? You been here most your grown days. Give it up, will you? Or, go back. Mercy sake, stop whining over that damn city.*

You know I can't go back, Lil stated. *I can't afford to live there. I barely get by down here.*

Listen to you, 'down here.' We're here,

Jeanette said, pointing to each of the women at the table. *New York is up there!* She pointed an index finger to the ceiling. *If you really wanted to be there, you would find a way. It is that simple.*

That simple my ass, Lil uttered sharply. *Nothing is that simple.*

Bull! Edith muttered.

Pardon? Lil asked.

You heard me, I said bull. You been talking about moving back to New York since Jack left, but you don't. Jeanette's right, maybe you don't really want to go. You just don't want to be Southern, that's all there is to it. Like there's something better about bein a Yankee, and we all know that's bull!

Bull in a china shop, Lil muttered, a way of describing Edith she has used often over the years, although more often endearingly.

They all met some forty years ago at an elementary school parents' meeting. Although classrooms had been integrated, black parents still clustered at back of the auditorium at the larger meetings. Conditioning, as well as safety in numbers. Edith, strikingly tall, dressed in a crisp linen pants suit, marched straight to the back, Jeanette, her stylish, peach-toned sister, close behind, wearing a revealing polka dot sundress that swished as she walked. All eyes watched as the two sat themselves down with a cordial nod to the black women seated in that row, cementing their reputations as locals who will defy expectations. Lil, who had recently moved to town, and down the street from Vera, attended the meeting for the first time, and, soon after that night, acknowledging the sisters' behavior as an act of grace, rather than grandstanding, their friendship was born.

Edith, language, please. And let's not be too hard on Lil, Vera said. *We all have a sense of place, don't we, and this just has never really been hers.*

Sense of place! Edith bellowed. *She settled here. Worked here all these years. Hell, you even stayed when you sold the house, you might have gone back then, we all thought you would. This is where you live, Lil. Your permanent landscape, a wildflower maybe, but you're dug in, like it or not. Maybe you ought to enjoy what time is left, before you actually do go to heaven.*

The truth is, Edith, it may have something to do with being black that you don't get, Vera proposed. *Isn't that so, Lil?*

Lil shrugged. *Some.*

What about being black? Edith asked.

Northern black is different from southern black, you know, Vera said.

Is that so? Jeanette asked.

Northern blacks are mostly from somewhere else, Lil explained. *Southern blacks, rooted here. That's what you mean, right?* she asked Vera.

Vera nodded.

Don't we all hail from somewhere else? Edith posed.

My people relocated north from states in the deep South. Migrants, they were, Lil said.

Migrants? Edith replied.

The great migration, Vera clarified. *Those who remained, we're indigenous, in effect.*

Lil laughed. *Indigenous? Let us not forget, we were shipped over here in the first place.*

Well… Vera started to say.

Migration is a choice, slavery was not, Lil snapped.

Okay, I've been misconstrued, Vera said, her voice dipping into the cajoling tone she used with the young children she once taught. *I meant to say, southern blacks landed here, not by choice, no, but our roots go many generations deep. Northern blacks, well, many, fled their roots in the migration, replanted in unfamiliar soil. What's that called when seeds are blown in the wind to foreign or inhospitable earth?*

Accidentals, Jeanette replied. *Birds carry*

seeds in their beaks too, from continent to continent.

Right, that's it, Vera said.

Well, you could argue southern blacks are the accidentals. Northerns chose their destination, Edith said.

Splitting hairs, Lil muttered. *My great-grandmother moved north from Alabama, that was the choice. I went backwards when I moved south.*

So, you belong there, not where your people are rooted? Edith asked.

I belong where I was raised. Maybe we all do, Lil answered.

This is giving me a headache, Jeanette griped. *I mean really, how many ways can you skin this fish? You make yourself belong where you are.*

Right you are, sister, Edith said. *Hundreds of years embedded in southern soil, hundreds of years adapting, as you put it, Vera, versus a few generations seeding the north? Still southern to the core, I would say.*

What a southern white woman would say, Lil growled.

This conversation is just plain nuts. I've lost the thread, Jeanette argued, and Edith chuckled.

The point is, a northern black, raised in the north, no longer fits in the south, but a southern black is a cotton tree. Rising, spreading. Deep roots, thick branches, Vera said, smiling sweetly.

That's it, right there, Lil bellowed.

But you chose to be here, Edith reiterated.

I did not, you know that. The company relocated Jack here and me with him.

So, you're like, what, a homeless person who decides to stay homeless? Edith cried.

No one decides to be homeless, Lil argued, with the authority of the social worker she was.

Those street people in San Francisco, and Portland, and even your precious New York, they won't go to shelters, they won't stay with families. They choose to be where they are, Edith argued.

No one wants to live on the streets, Lil insisted. *They know it's not always safe in shelters, they might get beat up or end up in jail anyway. And they're as tribal as the rest of us, maybe more so, they've been screwed by the system so often, they stick to who and what they know.*

Damned if they do, damned if they don't. Black or white, Vera said.

Okay, okay, but to stay, or go, try something else on, that's still a choice, Jeanette stated.

It's not a choice when other people make the decision for you, Lil countered.

I'll grant you that, Lil… Jeanette said.

Oh, thank goodness. I'm so grateful for your

blessing, Lil responded, with a hint of a smile, and Jeanette chuckled.

But no one is in your way now. Stay or go, your choice, just get on already, Edith argued.

Edith, must you be so very harsh? Vera pleaded. *We all have something we wish were different. Surely you can understand that.*

As one, their eyes and voices bowed to Vera's scold, as she leaned back in her chair, sipping her tea, as if the debate were officially ended, but then, as an afterthought, she leaned forward to pronounce, *however, I must say, Lil, the sisters have a point. Home is where the heart is.*

Amen! Edith thundered.

No place like home, Jeannette crooned.

Home is where we start from, Lil argued.

To their blank stares, she clarified. *DW Winnicott. Psychologist,* she said, wincing as she bowed her neck. *Got any Ben Gay, Vera?*

Sure, hon. I have some stuff from the natural store that does not smell so bad.

Vera touched Lil's hand like the landing of a tiny bird. The petite one, Vera is delicate boned, in contrast to plump Lil or the willowy Jeanette or the imposing Edith. She wears the same clothes every day that she wore to teach – dark skirts, white blouses, a cardigan sweater on her shoulders – as if to retain the identity.

She volunteers regularly at the library and tends the community garden. She takes stretching classes at the senior center and lunches, now and then, with friends. The prize of her week, she says, is the Wednesday night game of Hearts. More than one game, they play word games and memory games of their own design, adding spice to their camaraderie the way they add cinnamon or nutmeg to pastries: generously, and without measuring.

How's your grandson doing? Lil suddenly inquired of Edith.

Which one?

The one with the ADHD, Lil replied.

Edith shook her head. *Ants in his pants.*

Lil and Vera smiled, knowingly, having seen too often the refusal to accept fault lines in a child.

Honestly, all these labels these days, Edith argued. *ADD, OCD. Ridiculous. They are who they are and they're all different. He's a spirited child, that's all.*

Until he floods or beats up on his brother, Lil commented.

Lil never had children. She claimed she never wanted them, serving instead as a loving auntie, and dedicated to helping kids in need to survive, hopefully to thrive.

So he melts down sometimes. And brothers beat up on each other, that's the way it is, isn't that right? Edith contended.

Sisters sometimes too, Jeanette said, with a good natured poke to Edith's ribs.

He gets the support he needs with a special ed designation, Vera added.

Surely so. I just prefer a child with spunk. Will serve him well, Edith said.

They all nod at this, flicking and tossing cards as the game heats up and they play for a while, until Lil again stirs the pot of discord.

You want spunk, go to New York.

Sass, that's what spunk is up north, Edith murmured, just loudly enough to be heard.

How come when I'm talking to you, you miss half what I tell you, but Lil mutters under her breath and you hear just fine? Jeanette challenged her sister, with a smile.

Edith chuckled. *You are cruisin for the bruisin, dear girl.*

I watched Breakfast at Tiffany's again the other night, Lil said. *Audrey Hepburn cruising around New York in those gorgeous clothes…*

Lord, here we go, Jeanette groaned, laying

down her cards to stretch her arms and legs at once, like a cat unfurling after a nap in the sun, as graceful as the runway model she once was.

Time for a seventh inning stretch, I think, Edith said, rising to march around the room to the rhythm in her head.

Anyone need anything? Vera chirped.

Maybe some more chips, honey. This salsa hits the spot, Edith answered, licking lips as red and lustrous as freshly applied lipstick.

Edith has a hearty appetite for more than food – she's divorced three husbands over forty years, producing five children, all while working full time, and finally settled in with a fourth husband, who has a brood of his own. She joyfully assembles them all for holiday gatherings, amusing Jeanette, who has been married forty-five years to the same man, a man now stifled with dementia.

Home grown tomatoes, Vera said. *That's the secret, you know.*

I beg your pardon? Edith asked.

The salsa. Home grown tomatoes, the secret.

Crushed canned tomatoes works fine, the fire-roasted kind, and coarse chopped celery, I like it chunky, Jeanette said.

Vine ripened tomatoes make it sweeter, with

red onion, a little red pepper, and thick tomato juice, that's the ticket, Vera said.

Martha Stewart's got nothing on you! Lil remarked.

Wouldn't that be fun, Edith said. *To be a TV chef. A striking Southern senior citizen, sort of Rita Hayworth with a twang. Sounds rich, don't it?*

All four laugh uproariously, the tension of previous moments dispelled.

Rosalind Russell as Auntie Mame would be better, I think, Jeanette said, plopping on her chair and propping her hair like a movie star.

Katherine Hepburn, before the twitch, Lil said. *Golden Pond goes Carolina.*

Can you imagine Kate on a cooking show? Edith shrieked, laughter reverberating through her ample body.

Kate lived in a brownstone, due East of the theater district. Her bust was in the window, last time I was there, Lil said.

Her bust? Edith asked.

You know, a bronze bust.

Well, you make sure to send my warmest regards to Kate's bust when you go to New York, which I do hope will be soon, Edith grumbled.

The three shuffled cards and sipped their drinks, centering themselves again on the game, except for Lil, who sulked as she pulled her sweater off one shoulder to rub ointment along her neck. She took a deep breath, and another. *Is it hot in here all of a sudden?*

Maybe the ointment? Edith remarked.

You do look a bit flushed, dear, Vera said. *Here, sip some cold tea.*

She poured a glass for Lil, who took one sip and grimaced. *I'd rather the drink, but thanks,* she said, smiling at Vera, as she reached for her cocktail glass.

You're a bit old for the flashes, Jeanette chided, leaning toward Lil to take a closer look. *Actually, hon, your eyes are pretty bloodshot. Are you not sleeping? Too much G&T? Maybe lie down for a bit. We can take a break.*

Don't be silly. Just a little tired. Maybe some cold water Vera, please, Lil answered.

Of course, Vera said, jumping up and to the kitchen for the water, stopping on the way back to pluck a few ice cubes from the bucket on the sideboard.

Jeanette extended her long arms above her head, then bent down to touch her toes, like a yogi. *It's late, I suppose we should call it a night.*

I suppose, Edith remarked.

The night is still young, Vera argued.

Your hubbies must be hankering for you, Lil said, sarcastically, to Edith and Jeanette.

Hankering? That's rich, Edith countered. *Harry is buried in football. Or is it baseball tonight? An embarrassment of riches for couch potatoes.*

I thought baseball was a summer sport, Vera said.

Starts before spring and keeps on going, like the energizer bunny. One of these days, they'll be playing the World Series in Halloween costumes.

The three chuckled, while Lil focused on her breathing, quicker and shallower, fanning herself with her cards.

If it weren't for commercials, he might not even get up to pee. Might miss a touchdown, a homerun or a triple play. And then the replays must be seen! Edith said.

Louis, rest his soul, loved to go to the park to watch the minors, Vera said.

Vera was the first to bury a husband, six years ago, and she still sleeps on her side of the bed and leaves the light on in the hall, as if he is only working late.

Lil threw her husband out four years ago, when she suspected he'd been unfaithful and, when challenged, he did not deny. He refused to confess with whom, so she told him to leave. No discussion, no negotiation. Within days, he was out of the house and soon after, out of town. Lil may have salvaged her dignity, but she has never recovered from the betrayal, wearing her disenchantment on her sleeve, and suffering chronic headaches, as well as a form of paranoia that thrives in aggrieved women.

Husbands, Lil said, shaking her head. *Can't live with 'em, nor without 'em.*

Well, I guess I do both, don't I? Jeanette said. *Let's face it, he's there and not there. I could disappear and he'd not notice. Sometimes I wish I was the one who didn't know what was what.*

Vera patted Jeanette's hand and smiled. *Your marriage has lasted the longest, dear. Should be some comfort to that.*

Jeanette sighed. *Yes, there is that. It's just that we saved and planned, so many plans for when the kids were grown and the work was done, and he was so healthy, so strong, he seemed indestructible. Foolish, I know.*

Look at the bright side, sister. At least he's home. He wasn't much around for the longest time, leaving you to take care of everything, which you do so well, of course, Edith comforted.

Jeanette rubbed her eyes to press back the tears. *The strangest part is, the consummate salesman, who lived by his words, has few left.* She turned to Lil. *Really Lil, you should treasure your independence. A free agent. You can go anywhere, anytime, so by all means, go to New York, even if just to visit.*

What's the point of going on my own? Lil responded.

Edith scowled. *Enough, Lil. We give you room to moan for New York, but this persistent self-pity is just so tiresome. We've put up with it way too long. That's it, no more, you hear! And,* Edith continued, putting up a palm to Lil to refute a response, *no matter who Jack was sleeping with then. You're an unforgiving woman. Get over it.*

Lil and Edith glared at each other for a moment, until Lil turned away, unwilling to confront the disdain, and the truth, in her friend's eyes.

Edith rose from her chair to stand behind Jeanette, gently massaging her sister's shoulders. *At least Joe is always smiling these days,* she said. *No fuss, no temper, not yet.*

That's the truth. For now, Jeanette replied.

I suppose that's the only blessing of this hateful disease, Vera said. *He doesn't even know enough to be bothered by it.*

Praise the Lord, Edith roared, with a

bellowing sigh, as she returned to her seat.

Lil sat taller in her chair and scowled at her friends, like a defendant in court glowers at an accuser. Vera twisted a napkin in her hands into a knot, anxious at the hostility that has shrouded their game. Edith sipped her wine, senses on high alert. Jeanette sat starkly still, anger burning within, exasperated by Lil's unending self-indulgence, while she lives like an animal in a trap.

Truth is, Lil, I do know who was sleeping with Jack, but I'll never tell. Nothing would change for you, now would it? Jeanette said.

Edith reached over to place a hand on her sister's, who shook it off and went on, her anguish unleashed, in need of a target.

You don't deserve to know, just as you never deserved that sweet man. Maybe you will never go home again, at least not until you recognize that we are all tied to the lives we're given. No point blamin and whinin and cussin your fate. Until you accept that, you will never be at peace. No wonder you're pissy all the time. Nothing but misery in your heart.

Jeanette, please! Vera pleaded.

And you will not find what you think you need in New York, Jeanette shouted. *Wherever you go, darlin, there you are!*

Suddenly, staring at Jeanette in horror, Lil clutched her chest. *Oh!* she whimpered.

Good Lord, what now? Jeanette muttered.

What is it? Vera cried, reaching for Lil as she slumped face down to the card table, spittle dribbling from her lips. *Lil!* she screamed.

Call an ambulance, Edith instructed her sister, who stood frozen in place, terror in her eyes. *Right now, Jeanette!*

Edith gripped Lil's shoulders and lifted her from the table, leaning her gently against the chair. *Vera, get a wet cloth, will you? Lil honey, open your eyes. Can you hear me?*

Lil's eyes fluttered, then closed again. Perspiration veiled her face and her neck, her body slanted to one side like a drunk, as Edith struggled to hold her upright. *Jeanette, help me honey,* she called out to her sister, on the phone.

Hampton Boulevard. #22. White house at the end. Hurry! Jeanette cried.

Oh my God, Vera whimpered, stopped in the doorway with a wet washcloth in one hand. *What's happening to her?*

Hand it here, Edith said. *And help me get her to the couch. She should be prone.*

Should we move her? Jeanette asked.

What's happening? Vera repeated.

As Lil's limp body slanted toward the floor, Edith and Jeanette eased her into a safe position, and Vera placed a couch pillow under her head.

She's had too much to drink, Edith said.

I've seen Lil put away a lot more than that, Jeanette said.

You've upset her, Vera snapped.

I'd have upset her a lot more if I told her the truth, Jeanette argued.

Not the time, Jeanette, Edith commanded. *Damn, where is that ambulance?*

For a couple of moments, the three were fixed in place, tethered to Lil's fate. They wiped her brow and her neck, assuring her she was not alone, until a siren drew steadily louder, finally deafening, and a rotating red light flashed through the front window.

Vera jumped up to open the door for two emergency medical technicians, who glanced at the scene, then lifted Lil to a gurney, attached her to a portable EKG machine and covered her mouth with an oxygen mask that filled and deflated erratically, and then one inserted an IV as the other prepared a drip.

Vera slumped onto the couch, her arms wrapped across her chest, tears pouring down her cheeks. Edith scurried to her side, grasping her hands, while Jeanette hovered nearby, as if she might turn back the clock to take back her venomous rhetoric.

Don't think about it, Edith said to Vera.

I can't help it. I'm still so ashamed, she murmured.

It's over, Vera. Long ago. You were bereft after Louis died, it's no wonder… Edith said.

She was my friend and I betrayed her, Vera whined.

Lil was never satisfied with anything and Jack was unhappy. You leaned on each other, that's all, Jeanette said, joining them on the couch, and taking one hand of the sobbing Vera.

Jeanette looked up towards the gurney, attuned to the technicians' commands to each other as they reported heart rate, blood flow, breathing capacity. *Let her go,* she whimpered.

Jeanette! You don't mean that, Vera cried.

Let her go, Jeanette repeated. *What's the use of going on when you feel so stuck in place?*

Are you talking about Lil? Edith asked.

Jeanette shook her head sadly, for her friend, and for herself, as the three watched the technicians fight for a life force they knew, in their hearts, had slipped away years ago.

The Lil we know, the Lil we loved and played with and fought with, is already gone, Edith said.

A steady beep emanating from a small machine dropped suddenly to a continuous hum, accompanied by a flat fluorescent line on the monitor. Both technicians sprung into renewed fervor, attempting resuscitation.

They should leave her be now, Edith said. *There's nothing left for her here.*

Jeanette nodded.

I should have told her, when he left, Vera said, through her tears.

That's for confession, Jeanette said. *Would not have helped Lil, you know that. She thrived on disappointment, that's the truth of it. And while she may have been unhappy in this place, she loved us. Would have killed her to lose you, oh yes, that would have killed her far sooner.*

That's the damn truth, Vera, Edith said.

The technicians stopped. They checked watches, recorded the time and vital data into an electronic clipboard, then nodded apologies to the women on the couch. One wrapped up the equipment, while the other reported to the hospital that the subject had passed.

Edith stood and approached. *Give us a moment, will you?*

A moment, mam, he said, stepping aside.

The three friends circled Lil's lifeless body, in designated order, as if merely setting up another round of cards. Edith gently swept a few strands of moist hair from her forehead and cupped her still warm cheek.

Bye, old friend, Edith said, leaning close to whisper, *at last, my girl, your exile is over.*

Bless you, Vera murmured. *I will beg your forgiveness when we meet again.*

Rest in peace, Jeanette said. *I trust you'll find your place in the next place.*

They grasped hands and bowed their heads in silent prayer. The final hand, played. Hearts, intact. The formidable queen of spades, discarded for the win.

Customary Law

When the phone rang, splintering silence like sirens after midnight, Joanna was in bed, nestled against two pillows, a hardcover book pressed to her knees. The bedside clock in green glowing numerals read 8:32.

Everyone who knows her well knows she retires early to read, particularly when her husband, Dan, is working late, or out of town on business, which he is, frequently, still, albeit allegedly retired. Other than her two children, her sister and a few close friends, designated to break through the *do not disturb* on her phone, she will rarely pick up a call. In the dark hours, she argues, calls herald sadness or disaster. The death of a loved one. Another global tragedy. Hurting grandchildren. Only bad news knocks at night, she says.

Joanna is tall, long, she describes herself, with shoulder length hair the shade of polished silver, which she constantly brushes back from her eyes and behind her ears. The lines in her forehead are deeper than wrinkles around her eyes and lips, the consequence, she will say, of perpetual consternation. The type of woman one might mistake for a judge, which she is, often, although not from the bench.

Her legs, warmed in blue plaid flannel pajama pants, are elevated slightly on a white comforter folded at the foot of the king bed. A pastel blue shawl is draped over her shoulders and wire-rimmed magnifier glasses drift down her nose – the granny look, she says, although she disdains labels, particularly as progenitor, scoffing at contemporaries who forego their identities into monikers like Oma or Papa. Or Mom, for that matter. Her children were asked to call her by her given name, which they most always have. Only in distress, when they cried out, *please come, Mom. Help me, Mom*, her heart clutched in her chest and she rushed to their sides, what a mother, or grandmother will do, whatever they're called.

A pin light is clipped to the back cover of the book for better illumination and a pen is in hand. The novel she's reading, a deceptively simple story, follows a young slave girl who has escaped the historic Jamestown settlement only to brave horrific conditions in the wild.

Joanna admires the author, she's read all her earlier works, and eager to read on, despite a preponderance of road kill imagery.

This moment, the end of day, darkness close and reclined with a book, is a cherished moment, although these days, she can read any time she chooses, retired now from a thirty-five year career as an anthropology professor at the nearby Cal State. Old habits, however, stick, and reading for pleasure in daylight still seems profligate. Dan, on the other hand, who spends much of his time attending board meetings, or advising fledgling companies, prefers to read in a comfy chair in the den, and, most often, business journals. By the time he comes to bed, Joanna is asleep, the pleasure of rest and literature a tonic, much as she once read herself to sleep when she was a girl.

Whenever she urges Dan to read a well told story in the evening, a bit of fiction, she will nudge, he argues he needs to stay current in a rapidly changing economic climate. She believes he simply cannot still his mind; he has always been so.

If more business people read fine literature, they might better understand the human condition, and might, as a result, be better business people, she is known to pontificate. *Storytelling is the path to expanding one's world view, and will go a long way to enhance corporate compassion.*

Dan rarely debates the point, because he avoids avoidable conflict, and he knows she's right. They both have learned to choose their battles, the hallmark of a long marriage.

All a matter of trade-offs, she tells her now grown children, who have both recently found partners, something particularly gratifying to Joanna, like the perfect coda to a classical music masterpiece. Or, closing each day in bed with a good book.

For some reason, perhaps a sense of portent, when the phone rang this night, she glanced at the screen, and when she saw it was her friend Loren calling, she answered.

Hey, you're home early. How'd it go?

There was a moment of hesitation on the other end and a choke in Loren's voice.

Joanna tossed the book aside and sat up in alarm. *Loren? Are you all right?*

I'm sorry to call so late, did I bother Dan?

It's not late, and he's away.

Again?

Yes, again, what's happened?

I was waiting at the back entrance off the

parking lot at the hotel, as agreed… She paused.

Loren, are you hurt?

Nothing physical, no, no, but I saw him, Jo. He drove slowly by, canvassing, sort of, before the date, and he came so close, I nearly called out to him, and then, he just kept going and sped away.

Are you sure it was him?

Yes. I've seen his photos. We had a video chat. He told me he drove an Audi. Silver. It was him. I'm sure of it. He just didn't like what he saw.

There must be another explanation. Did he send a message?

No. I checked. And I waited, maybe fifteen minutes, mostly to calm down, although, I thought, I don't know, I thought, maybe he had an errand he'd forgotten. Maybe he went to buy me flowers. What an ass I am.

You are not an ass. Something must have happened. Where are you?

In the car. Driving around. I couldn't bear to go home. I bought a new sweater. I'm wearing perfume. I feel like the girl no one asked to dance at the prom. Silly, I know…

Nothing silly about it. Come here. I'm up. We'll have an after-dinner drink.

You're in bed with a book.

I'm getting out of bed as we speak. Come.

Are you sure?

Absolutely. I'm wearing a raggy sweatshirt and you'll have to confront my naked face.

Not the first time.

Nor the last.

I'll be there in a few. Thank you.

Bastard, Joanna grumbles, climbing off the bed and fluffing the pillows for her return. The older they are the worse, as if entitled to a good woman's affection. Like several of Dan's colleagues who have betrayed marriages for younger flesh, as if they have so much to offer by virtue of an impressive business title or academic credentials. A spiffy car. They tout memberships at an exclusive gym or country club, as if historic achievements.

Cretins, she mutters, although Dan is not a cretin, only fussier with age and often absent.

Ten years ago, as they were adjusting to their emptying nest, they barely survived a volcanic disruption. The mountain rising from too many mole hills. Dan moved out for a few months and they both thought their marriage had run its course. Joanna wondered then, and again, tonight, if he trolled online for someone new. She never asked. She'd rather not know. In the end, they returned to each other, not so much working through what ailed them, but trashing their disappointments in favor of their vows. Tethered by endurance. Dan has been known to say, particularly when Joanna is in earshot, she is a superlative woman and he'd be a fool to dip a toe into another pond. She appreciates the sentiment. Still, like many elder women, she fears the greener grass. On the other hand, the people they know who have plowed into the snarl of internet mating, all tell stories, often humorous, and others, what she suspects Loren encountered tonight, appalling. Joanna is quite certain that if her marriage collapsed, she would prefer what her divorced sister calls *tyrannical solitude* to the labyrinth people put themselves through in a desperate quest to avoid aloneness.

After all, as she likes to remind friends, anthropologists determined more than a century ago, and Darwin expanded upon in his treatise on evolution, that while mammals and related classes mate, some for life, the purpose of the union is the perpetuation of the species. Sexual attraction, eroticism, merely a carnal imperative. Pleasure is not what binds.

Beyond that, in this era of longer lives, no one should be shocked by so many later life divorces, nor plummeting marriage rates. Few marriages can be sustained fifty, sixty, maybe seventy years. For most, there is a shelf life.

Lord, the human race long ago lost the race, she grunts, an expression that used to tickle her students.

She cautions herself to put on a better face in order to shore up dear Loren, who keeps going back to the dating well over and over again. Something like Albert Einstein's theory of madness: engaging repeatedly in the same behavior, expecting a different outcome.

In the kitchen, she digs into a cabinet where she stores liqueurs and grabs Bailey's, also a bottle of Cointreau, both sweet, soothing, she hopes, then up on her toes to reach into a higher shelf for aperitif glasses. She's had on her project list for a while to cleanse her kitchen of paraphernalia rarely used; however, in this moment, she's glad she has what suits.

Loren, a prototype for graceful aging, arrives with bloodshot eyes, cheeks smudged with mascara, otherwise meticulous, as if she were dressed by a costume designer, a career she once explored. Instead, she earned a license in real estate, her look as curated as a property staged for sale. A gold cashmere V-neck lands at slim hips, chocolate suede pants hug tapered legs, and she stands on espresso leather ankle boots on a stacked heel. Exquisitely autumnal. Nothing like the long black skirts and billowy blouses Joanna wore for years, and the black leggings and floppy sweaters she lives in now.

Loren's hair is as auburn as in her youth, cascading to her jaw. Deep brown eyes tinted taupe on the lids and her cheeks with a peachy blush. She wears a thick gold choker, accenting a willowy neck, like a Modigliani. She confided once to Joanna she thought the neck the sexiest part of a woman's body. *The greatest turn on for me is when a man kisses my neck,* she remarked, and then blushed with embarrassment, as if she had divulged a pornographic fantasy.

Joanna responded then with an esoteric factoid about island cultures where the natives, under duress, wrap their hands around their necks, interlocking fingers at the tender spot where the neck hits the chest, the suprasternal notch, which, to many indigenous peoples in the Pacific, is considered the seat of the soul. The spiritual and the sensual entwined. Loren stared at her that day, bewildered by the commentary, then reminded Joanna, kindly, as good friends have over the years, her children as well, that such details may be fascinating, but irrelevant to the moment.

She makes a mental note not to sound like a pedagogue tonight.

When Loren arrives, when Joanna pulls her into a warm hug, she feels skeletal, more than usual, painfully thin bodies in the mating culture meant to suggest she doesn't need much, not even feeding. She has often felt compelled to remind friends that females long ago carried extra padding in their hips and thighs, and coveted for it. Amazonian women, in fact, were deemed goddesses.

She holds Loren a bit longer to soothe, a moment too long, as Loren begins to weep, her defenses let down in the comfort of kindness.

I'm sorry. I'm being a dolt, Loren whines, as she pulls away and reaches for a crumpled tissue in her jacket pocket. *I just thought, after we talked, this guy, he seemed so great.*

You are not a dolt, no matter what you're feeling at this moment. Come, Joanna instructs, leading Loren to the kitchen, where she grabs a bowl of red grapes from the refrigerator to cushion the liqueur.

I've lost my appetite, Loren mutters.

Eat something with the drink.

Have you got a sweet?

I'll search the freezer. I'm limiting sugar.

I do not exist without sugar.

Joanna smiles. At the worst of times, her friend retains a sense of humor.

She drops cubes into their glasses and Loren pours Bailey's into hers, attending to the crackling of the ice with a cock of her head, as if a music box, and then she sips, mulling the flavor before she swallows.

Mm, delicious, she coos, and sips again.

Joanna has discovered frozen brownies in the freezer, which she plops on the counter, unfolding the foil to present.

Really Jo. I've had more than my share of bad first dates, as you well know, but I've never been so humiliated, Loren whimpers.

Seriously? For some inexplicable reason, he decided not to meet you after all. You don't even know this guy. You cannot let him decide your worth? Be rational! Shall I microwave these?

Better cold, Loren answers, breaking off half a brownie and holding between a thumb and forefinger, like a jewel.

I know it's irrational. Totally emotional. But rejection never gets easier. You would avoid all this, I know, but I need to be in the arena, embrace my vulnerability, as Brené Brown says.

Loren honors the platitudes of the gurus of self-care and self-actualization and Joanna does not correct her that Teddy Roosevelt first coined that terminology.

So you're devoured by lions, Joanna says.

Loren takes another sip of her drink and a bite of the brownie, smacking her lips with pleasure.

Like Ulysses, Joanna thinks, and quotes aloud, *…a ripe and luscious vine, hung thick with grapes.*

What?

The Odyssey. I'm about to tackle the new translation with a study group.

Of course you are, Loren mutters.

Joanna does not take offense. She's often mocked for intellectual pursuits. Also because she spits opinions like olive pits. Everything exists within an evolutionary context, she will say, like an enduring friendship. Together, she and Loren have cheered or wept for their children, friends and husbands, poured hearts out over hundreds of cups of coffee, and attended, although reluctantly, too many PTA meetings, where Joanna derided what she called *the mad hatters,* the parents who took everything *oh so seriously*, until a school board member spouted regressive rhetoric about books, and Joanna turned into a madder hatter.

Loren takes the last bite of the brownie and reaches for her phone. *He sent a message.*

Took long enough, Joanna gripes.

He says something came up he had to deal with, he's so sorry he couldn't meet after all. But he was there, I swear.

So, he's a liar, as well as a cretin, Joanna says. *You're well free of him.*

Loren shakes her head, sadly. *He didn't seem that sort of guy, Jo.*

You never know.

I suppose. My radar is usually good, and this one seemed so real. More grounded than the others I've talked to. Looks much younger than he is too. Where's your computer?

In the den, why?

I want you to take a look at his profile.

You told me about him.

Yes, but please, take a look. Help me see what I missed.

Maybe he's been dishonest, nothing more to see. Maybe he's just a brute.

I don't think so. Indulge me, please, Loren pleads, pointing in the direction of the den.

Okay, but only if you eat a little something more. You're withering away.

I'm not, but okay, I will. These are your best batch yet, she calls out, as Joanna makes her way down the hall to retrieve the laptop.

Joanna chuckles. She's not much of a baker, but chocolate always pleases. Loren was better at all of it: seamstress, chef, soother. When she discovered her husband of nearly forty years was involved with another woman, Joanna was the friend she stayed with for two weeks, unwilling to be seen in the light of day, as if she were the pariah.

She was totally blind-sighted, she said. Their kids were graduating. Their lives seemed on track. There were challenges, she conceded, and she presumed the longer absences were medical emergencies or protracted surgeries, hardly a serious relationship, which made the infidelity all the more heinous.

She told Joanna she might have tolerated a fling. *Some aging men need a reboot.* But then, he filed for divorce.

The emotional whiplash mutated into something like PTSD and, ever since, Loren has been obsessively determined to replace him, internet dating the matchmaker of the age.

I'll log in, Loren says, a dab of chocolate on her fingertips, which she wipes off first with a napkin. *Here he is,* she proclaims, heaving a deep sigh. *Jason is his name.*

Joanna scans his photo. Yes, pleasing, in an all-American way. Weathered charm. Deep wrinkles at the eyes, like an outdoorsman. A firm jawline, squat neck. Graying shaggy hair. One of those men who age into merely an older version of the boy they were.

How old? she asks.

Seventy.

Maybe.

I think he told the truth.

Divorced or widowed?

Widowed. Less baggage.

Didn't you say widowers are looking for a substitute wife?

If they haven't been alone long, that's true, but they aren't as cynical. They still like women.

Men who like women always like women, Loren. They are sexual beings, first to last.

Okay, but you know what I mean, Loren grumbles, petulant in her defense.

I do. So, besides boyish good looks, what's the appeal?

He's a retired professor, like you.

Joanna laughs. *Well, that explains it. We know how tiresome academics are. What field, do you know?*

Sociology. Kindred spirit, yes?

Yes and no.

How so? I suppose I should know this, but I only took 101, Loren says, with a shrug.

Simple, really. Cultural anthropologists, like me, study prior civilizations to better frame the future. Sociology examines the structure of societies and their interaction. Present tense.

Loren nods, clearly befuddled, the sort of expression Joanna saw too often in her students' eyes, so she decides to share a little known fact to lighten the load.

Here's an interesting tidbit, perfect for a cocktail party or a first date. Margaret Mead was a crucially important, and arguably most renowned anthropologist, despite questions over her methods, but did you know, Karl Marx is one of the founders of sociology?

The communist? Loren asks, shocked, as people are, when they learn this.

Socialist actually. A theorist. Philosophical anthropology was his thing, fascinated by human relations, most notably, alienation, which he believed would be ameliorated by collectivism. I have to wonder what old Karl would think of internet dating.

Joanna chuckles, but Loren has lost her sense of humor, staring dejectedly at the photo on the screen.

The thing is, he does not seem at all tiresome. He plays tennis, he plays chess. He loves jazz. He volunteers at a food pantry. He's devoted to his kids and grandkids.

When Loren's eyes tear up, Joanna pats her hand, then turns the laptop toward her to better scan the cascade of images, because she knows Loren wants her to.

A robust older man wearing a tuxedo at a wedding. Dressed in white shorts, revealing muscular legs and brandishing a tennis racket. Seated at a picnic table with a group his age, champagne glasses raised for a toast. A series of photos with three fresh-faced young adults, likely his kids, given the glowing smile, and another, a selfie with them all in his embrace. He seems decent enough, Joanna would agree, although images belie truth, particularly on the internet. If he is the sort of stand up person he seems, why would he have fled seconds before contact, and then make a lame excuse?

My friend, he may be a true narcissist. Hard

Loren nods, grateful for the solidarity. When she downs a second glass of the liqueur, she goes mushy, then weepy, so Joanna insists she spend the night in the guest room, where she sleeps late and awakens groggy.

After two cups of coffee, barely nibbling the oatmeal Joanna has prepared, Loren heads home, tail still between her legs.

Joanna, however, stews on the situation, too angry on her friend's behalf to let it go. Any man who preys on an innately good woman, like Loren, should be made to suffer the same. She decides to hunt for him online with the sole purpose of avenging her friend, justifying her intent as a micro-ethnographic study of elder mating habits.

The day is damp and chilly, early fall weather common to southern New England. Joanna is happily home in warm cushy clothes. Classical piano emanates from a speaker on a bookshelf in the den, where she sits at the desk to set up an account on the matchmaking site. Once she gets through the navigation and signs up for a trial period, she invents a handle, Prof, and posts the best photo she can find, which Loren, ironically, snapped when they attended a friend's birthday party last year.

Staring at herself on screen, she can see how much she's aged. Deeper etching around eyes and lips. Hollowed cheeks. In photos, her hair looks nearly white. She may be on a fool's journey – men her age surely prefer younger women with pillowy cleavage, lush lips, come hither smiles. Or women, like Loren, who seem younger than they are. If this ruse is to work, the mark, she thinks of him, will have to be a sapiosexual. She's always been more attractive for her brain than her body.

She hesitates, briefly, but determination to exact vengeance for her sweet friend, for any woman prey to such heartlessness, keeps her going. She fills in the details. Age, 68. Retired professor, she does not specify her field. She checks off a woman seeking a man, surprised by the long list of options. Hobbies, tennis and chess, although she hasn't been on a tennis court in ten years and is at best an amateur at chess. She prefers Go. She lists jazz as favored music, although she hasn't been to a jazz club in ages. She clicks travel as a pastime. *Duh,* she mutters. She almost adds long walks on the beach, but she will not sink to that cliché.

In seconds, the algorithm kicks in and she's presented with a surprisingly long list of candidates. She laughs loudly as she scans the hyperbolic commentary, the rhetoric contrived and disingenuous.

Utter madness, she mutters.

In all this cyber-nonsense, she knows, the tacit promise of happily ever after.

When she quits for the night, she cannot focus on reading. She's beset with the question of how and why mature men and women fawn over strangers, transmitting winks or seductive messages, making themselves the target of bad actors, not to mention repeated rejection. She might use what she learns as a thesis for an article, if only to better occupy the hours while Dan wanders across the country preserving his potency. She's still in touch with a few editors who might welcome an investigation into first world, late-age mating rituals.

The next morning, she finds a handful of introductory messages, one from the ex-husband of a neighbor, another from a former colleague, who says he had no idea she was single and would like to catch up. She realizes she should have been more discreet. She would not want Dan to get wind of this before she fills him in, although, how would he know?

She makes a mental note to tell him all about it as soon as he gets home tomorrow.

She tweaks her profile to better appeal to Jason, the perpetrator, uploading a slightly younger photo and adding additional bites of innocuous personal information.

The next day, he responds.

Let the game begin, she cries in triumph.

What field, he asks in his first text.

Similar, but not, she says, intentionally elusive, because men prefer a chase and cyber-space facilitates mystique.

Would you like to chat first? Before a face to face. Or are you game for a video visit? Not that I look any better on screen, but there it is.

What she wants to say is, let's skip the pretense of self-effacement, I'm on to you, but she does not. She lets him wait until, after a while, she replies that she prefers a phone call.

We all suffer Zoom fatigue these days. And it takes time to reveal oneself under these artificial circumstances. We can speak through the app, safer as well, he responds.

A surprisingly thoughtful response.

Perhaps this is how he reels women in. She wonders again what could have happened that night to make him drive off, but she'll never know, because she plans to teach him the error of his ways by arranging the same logistics and driving off the same. An eye for an eye.

She writes back a time the following day and he sends a thumbs up.

Dan calls to report he has to stay another day for an extended meeting.

We don't have anything pressing on the calendar, right?

She has no reason to doubt her husband; she's merely disappointed. She hoped to tell him sooner than later what happened, and the payback she plans for the offender. They will share a laugh, share the outrage, although Dan is inclined to defend fellow men. Right now, however, he seems rushed, so she decides to defer the conversation until he's at home. Until she has his full attention and she can tell the whole story, with the punchline.

In Greek lore, Jason was celebrated as a healer, and a savior, although his mythological counterpart seduced Medea in order to help him restore his throne, and then he abandoned her. Named accordingly, Joanna thinks now, which strengthens her resolve.

At the appointed hour, he calls. He has a deep voice, a voice of authority, although he stammers nervously at the start. Not quite the arrogant academic she expected. Reminds her of the first time her son asked a girl on a date. His tender heart. The threat of rejection. Young and old, male and female, toes dipped in hot water, braving the burn.

So, we are both scholars, he says, steering the conversation to common ground.

Extensively published, she replies, with matching conceit.

He chuckles. *I have to admit, I never had a passion for the publishing. I preferred the classroom. Those inquiring minds. Their delight, the good ones, in study. Did you feel that way?*

Yes, of course, she agrees. *Although I like research, and the writing. Material taking shape in a meaningful way.*

She almost says, I am good at scoping out the truth.

He asks about grandchildren. He has six, he proclaims proudly.

Just like their parents. Inquisitive, spirited. One, the eldest, has a label, he confides. *Social anxiety disorder. To me, he's special, sensitive, not inadequate. I don't want this to define him.*

Joanna is discomfited by his candor. She's always been easily flustered by strangers who puncture her natural reserve. She would rather such a reveal were relegated to the right time and place, to a trusted listener.

To her silence, he goes on.

My wife, may she rest in peace, was a better parent. I was always at odds with which way to go, so I followed her lead. I just made sure the kids knew I had their backs. That's all a dad can do. And a granddad. Like a tribal chief, right? Wise and kind.

She appreciates the reference. *But you were co-parents, were you not?*

She was the better interpreter. I lean to the bilateral argument. I read all the parenting experts, much good that did me. My kids were excellent at arguing me out of most anything.

He chuckles and she cannot help but smile at his unassuming humor.

Joanna asks, surprising herself as well as him, *tell me something about yourself that has nothing to do with your tenure. Or being a parent. Who are you beyond the academic?*

Hmm, a true anthropologist. Cultural?

Yes, she says, peeved to be summarily

labeled. She may be more transparent than she thinks, or meant to be, and she cautions herself to stay on guard.

With little contemplation, as if her query has tapped into something that weighs on his mind, he replies.

I don't speak of this often, but to answer the question truthfully, I was the eldest of three kids, but not the first born. I had a brother, two years older, who died of polio before he got to school. I have no memory of him, just a handful of photos. Still, I've always felt a vacancy. Hard to explain. I do think these things inform who we are.

Joanna, speechless, recalls a mystery she watched not long ago, in which a litigator tells a junior lawyer never to ask a question without being prepared for the answer. In this case, she was completely unprepared, and feels badly to have perhaps pierced a wound.

Maybe a bit too personal too soon, he says, to her silence.

No, no, my apologies. Now she's the one stammering. *I didn't mean to go so deep into the personal. An investigative nature. Mea culpa.*

Which I appreciate, of course. And a fair question. As I said, I don't think about it much.

You might reasonably wonder if that feeling

you describe underscores your search for a match.

We're all here to connect, to fill some sort of an emotional void, whatever our unique history.

Yes, of course, she concedes.

So, your turn. What do you wish to share?

Well, if we're talking childhood memories, what comes to mind is when I was a twelve I was a babysitter, she replies, and smiles remembering. *I resented that it was the only way I could earn money at the time, but that sense of responsibility has proven invaluable.*

I get it. At that age, I was mowing lawns, and by knowing my neighbors, their pride in their homes and gardens, something of an introduction to ethnography. Societal norms. Group aspiration.

Your first qualitative study.

Exactly! Although nowadays, hard to trust anything but the empirical…

Even then, she interjects.

100 percent, as my kids say. Aging, I mean, where I am right now, makes me determined to let go of absolutes. Uncertainty is the better metric.

How right he is, and how satisfying to converse again with a scholar.

You know, when I was a girl, I tried to join neighborhood boys in play, but was usually rejected. Ostensibly because I was not athletic.

But you play tennis, he says.

Badly, she replies, and he laughs.

Like breaking into the academic fortress, he says. *You had to learn early on the boys club can be formidable. I should apologize for all of us.*

Thank you. I've waited years for that, she says, and they both laugh. *However, like it or not, that served as an initiation into the study of the communal. Like lawnmowing.*

Precisely.

As pleasant as the conversation is, she feels a tight knot deep in her gut she feels when she's behaving badly. A warning she relies on, although she ignores it. She's being dishonest, yes, but she's on a mission, and, right now, the discourse is stimulating.

My older daughter is pursuing a doctorate now, in philosophy, no comment, and starting a family at the same time, he says. *Her husband, partner I should say, says he will share the load, although I'll believe that when I see it. We don't have a good track record.*

Yes. I mean no, she responds.

He chuckles. *She faces an arduous path ahead, as you know. The challenges of academia. I'm glad that's in my rear view mirror. Even as we look back longingly at lost youth, I'm liking where I am.*

The unscheduled calendar. Reading for pleasure. Catching up with old friends. Doing what we never had time for when we were serving tenure. In this, age is an asset, don't you think?

Age is an asset like any other asset. Depends on how well it's used.

Well said. So, here's the thing, he says. *I've been on my own five years now, since I lost my wife. I think I was clear about that in the posting.*

Yes. I am sorry for your loss.

Kind of you. I miss her, of course. I miss the companionship or I wouldn't be here, and I'm sure my late wife is giggling at this crazy internet thing. Mostly I miss, well, I miss the intimacy, and by this I mean emotional as well as physical. I'm pretty sure you're new to this site or I would have spotted you sooner. So, tell me, what are you after? As attractive and interesting as you are, and you are, I'm looking for something, well, something that will last. I'm not a frivolous man. Sowed my oats a long time ago. He sighs. *Sorry. Maybe this is a conversation to be had over a glass of wine. Shall we meet?*

Joanna feels like a conquering hero – the first step deftly navigated. On the other hand, she has the nagging feeling she's convicted an innocent man. She prides herself on being a good judge of character and nothing about him seems Machiavellian. Even more disconcerting is that she feels something she hasn't felt in longer than she can remember: the pleasure of getting to know an interesting man. A man with common interests. Their chat is a means to an end, but the means are quite pleasing.

She gazes at his profile on her computer screen, and he seems, again, as he did at first, a stand-up guy. Nevertheless, she will teach him a lesson. That's the point. She proposes to meet the next night at the hotel bar where the deed was done, where she will exact her revenge.

The hotel your hunting ground? he asks.

Oh no. I am new at this, but it's a place, I, I was told, a good place to meet, I hear, she sputters.

It is popular, yes. Lively. Less isolating for a woman, for sure. And the bar food is not bad.

Your hangout? she quips.

No, just a couple of times. I'm not a lothario, I'm just, well, I am searching. Tomorrow too soon? Five? Carry a book, to make sure I don't accost another attractive woman by mistake.

I always carry a book, she says, ignoring the compliment.

I'm sure you do, he says.

Joanna hears a grin in his voice and she pictures his smile. Again, she fears there's been a rush to judgment. Nevertheless, the die is cast. She will finish what she's started. Teach him a lesson he will hopefully never forget.

She sleeps fitfully, like an adolescent girl before a first date, more so because she failed to suggest they meet at the back door, the scene of the crime. She should have prepared better, she scolds herself. She will have to admonish him face to face.

She fusses the next day over what to wear and how to present. She pulls a knit V-neck dress from the back of the closet, saved for an occasional business gathering. Marine blue brings out the blue in her eyes. She's relieved it fits, even if snug over wider hips. She applies light foundation to her face, a touch of blush to her cheeks and mascara to the eye lashes, and sprays rose water on her neck and down into the décolletage, the scent sweet and seductive. She lets her freshly washed hair fall to her shoulders, then steps back to gaze at her image in the mirror. Aged, but not elderly, and not unattractive. Good enough.

I should dress up more often, she thinks. I should dress for Dan. Dress to feel desirable. They should get out more. Find a cozy jazz club. Get sexy. Reclaim their youthful passion.

Jason has sent her his cell phone number in case she's running late or has to change the date. She does not return the favor. She does not want him to be able to track her down after he's been taught his lesson.

On the way out the door, she hesitates. She could stay home and stand him up. Delete her profile and then fall off the radar. Mission accomplished. After all, payback, also known as customary law, has been a tribal tradition since the beginning of time. On the other hand, she wants him to acknowledge his crime.

She propels herself to the car and to the hotel, where she will take the full measure of him, explicate the outrage, and then, flee.

The dimly lit bar anchors an atrium in one of the upscale brands of the Marriott chain. To either side, wide arches flank staircases to guest rooms, where windows, like a series of shadow boxes, overlook the open space below, as if prodding guests to commune. Flickering candles invite intimacy. Conversation thrums in low tones. Clinking glasses and ice cubes set the mood, jazz a background soundtrack. The sort of place where liaisons bloom. Deals close. Passion wafts through the air, like smoke.

Arriving early, she glances around, and

then straightens her shoulders for battle, an avenging militia of one. She's surprised to find Jason already at a table for two tucked to the side. He waves to her and as she makes her way toward him, she notices on the table a hard cover copy of an anthology of writings by Ruth Benedict, the cultural anthropologist cast into the shadow of Margaret Mead and compatriots. Joanna has written extensively about her, often citing her egalitarian mentality to her students. At first glance, she assumes the book is a maneuver to impress; however the binding is creased and pages flagged, the marks of a close reading.

She straightens her shoulders and lifts her head high, preparing for battle. As he stands to greet her, he reaches out for her hand. His is warm and strong. He's only a few inches taller than she. Sturdy, not foreboding. She's relieved he's not looming, as she thought he might be, not having checked his stats as well as she might have. He wears a navy blue crew neck sweater, the collar of a pastel blue shirt peeking out. Pressed weathered jeans. He's freshly shaved, skin tinged by the sun, and the jowl along the jaw softer than in his photos. His smile is the smile of a kindhearted headmaster.

Hardly predatory.

Then again, she knows, narcissists can charm the pants off even the most guarded women and serial killers were often attractive.

What is it about a bar or a café late in the day that feels like a sanctuary? she asks, as she withdraws her hand and sits.

A sanctuary? Ah, like a hub for the weary traveler. Nice metaphor. Although these spaces are contrived to curry confidence and favors. Perfect for spies, don't you think?

Marx would think it a laboratory for human interaction.

He laughs, appreciably. *Only a woman in the know would know that.*

Humans fulfill themselves through their creations, so what they make is an expression of what they are, she quotes. *I think I have that right.*

I think you do. What's your preference? he asks, as he hands her the menu and wine list.

They agree to share a pinot noir and he suggests root vegetables with hummus as well. She nods agreeably. As a server drops off tall glasses of water, they appraise each other.

She has heard that previous marriage is a common theme on a first date, the need for commiseration like comfort food. Thankfully, he doesn't ask, because she has not until this moment fabricated a relationship history or the lies she will tell in the interest of justice. She points to the book instead and asks if he's a fan of Benedict, and he responds, fluidly, about the circle of anthropologists who paved the way to sociology.

I recently re-read a biography written by Frank Boas, you know it, I'm sure, he says.

One of Joanna's idols. *Giants in the field, on the front lines of the greatest moral battle of our time. I believe the term was undivided.*

Exactly. From the biological to the cultural, from nature to nurture. I'm paraphrasing, of course.

Close enough, she says, with a nod.

Of course, I'm not telling you anything you don't know. I wouldn't want to be a mansplainer. I would not want to sound like the bore I can be. My daughter has cautioned me once too often on this.

She laughs. *I'm accused of the same.*

The waiter delivers a carafe of wine at the same time as a server conveys a bubbling terrine of cruciferous vegetables, with a bowl of hummus. As Jason pours wine, Joanna doles out a portion of the vegetables for him, and one for herself, with generous spoonful's of the dip.

They move in tandem, as if they've done

this many times before.

When he holds up his glass, she follows, and, with a clink, he says, *a pleasure to meet you*.

She smiles, and then, suddenly starving, having skipped lunch, as well as needing to settle her anxiety, she dives into the starter and sips wine, sighing with satisfaction as she relaxes into the ambiance.

She cannot ignore the unexpected thrill of an assignation. He's right, she thinks. This bar is a perfect place for a spy, or an avenger.

I watched an interesting film on Kanopy the other night… he says.

Joanna nods. University faculty have exclusive access to the site. *Which?* she asks.

Tomorrow, the documentary. Seen it?

A former colleague urged me to watch, because I'm too much an ostrich lately about climate change. A runaway train, I'm afraid, she laments.

Sadly so, but what a feat of filmmaking. Avoided the usual doom and gloom.

Sometimes I wish I were still teaching. Not the logistics, no, but, well, the farther removed from youthful optimism, the harder to maintain hope.

This feeling has been weighing on her, although she's not yet shared it with anyone.

I get that. The students, not the deadlines.

I'll drink to that, she says, and they raise their glasses again and sip.

I do see my grandchildren more often, which is great, and I feel a sort of liberation I've not felt since, well, not since I was very young. You know, unencumbered, so to speak, he says.

She nods, and he nods.

He smiles, and she smiles.

They sip again, nibble vegetables, and go on chatting, amiably, as if they've known each other a long time, or were meant to, and as they do, Joanna has the sudden sobering realization Loren was all wrong for Jason. The algorithm is faulty. Her friend is bright and attractive, and will be a loving partner. This man, however, requires a woman who shares the passionate pursuit of knowing. A woman who shares context. She would be the better match, a revelation as shocking as unsettling. She would no less wish to betray her friend than her marriage. Nonetheless, every one of her senses is on alert and a sublime sexual charge is surging through her body.

To defuse her jitters, she reaches for a bite of food, eyes lowered. He watches her as if she's a participant in a study and, when she looks up, when their eyes meet, his, piercing, are lit with desire. A magnetic field electrifies the space between them.

No, this cannot be, Joanna argues with herself. This should be the moment to deliver the punch. She must not falter, yet she cannot seem to say what she's come to say.

He leans toward her, as if he senses her discord, and as he does, she is further seduced by his scent: sandalwood. Earthy. Sensory. An old-fashioned fragrance correlated to youthful infatuation. She shakes her head to shake away these bizarre feelings, and then, struck back to reality by an admonishing wind, she stiffens, thrusts her back against her seat to establish a proper distance, and tells him exactly why she's here with him.

Oh no, he cries. *I felt just awful that night. Appalled by my behavior. Wait… that's the reason you're here? A sort of ghosting, I've heard of that, but, well, I guess I'm a babe in these woods.*

You are the one who ghosted her! She was standing there, waiting to meet you, all dressed up. Hopeful. You shamed her, Jason.

He freezes, scolded into silence, before presenting an argument in his defense.

Of course, yes, it seems that way. Please, let me explain. I want you to know. Loren should know as well. I'd seen her photo. One of those thumbnails we post on match sites. And then, cropped on Zoom, on my iPad. She's an attractive woman, for sure, and she seemed lovely. But when I drove in that night, she was standing at the back door, and in that light, an overhead lamplight, she looked like my late wife. I mean, exactly like her. An apparition. Tears fill his eyes. *The same body type. Narrow, bony, in fact, the way my wife was toward the end. The same deportment. Classy. Trusting. I freaked out. I'm not proud of this. I fled, like literally being chased by a ghost. And then I couldn't find the words to explain. I felt terrible. I should have called. I should have told her the truth. Please, forgive me.*

When Joanna, stunned by what he has said, does not respond, he presses his case.

I would never do such a thing intentionally. Unforgivable, I know, and I will fall on my knees to Loren to beg forgiveness.

The damage is done, Joanna retorts.

Please. He reaches for her hand and she lets him take it. *Something is happening between us. A rare immediate connection. Beyond collegial. Let's not give up over an odious mistake. Tell me what to do to make this right and I will. Whatever it takes, I will do.*

Joanna has come to teach him the error

of his ways and she has, and she realizes she cannot spend another moment with this man. She feels shockingly vulnerable. Yielding. She has not felt such an intense visceral response since her first love, nor since Dan, so long ago.

She shakes her head no, with profound sadness. Giving up on what she could not have possibly anticipated.

We have no compassion and we ask no compassion from you. When our turn comes, we shall not make excuses for our terror, he recites.

A quote from Karl Marx.

She deserves this. She's been cruel. She gathers her things to get away.

The deed is done.

I'll walk you to the car, he says.

Although Joanna is desperate to dispel the hold he seems to have on her, she waits for him to settle the bill, and together they make their way through the hotel passage to the rear door, back to the scene of the crime, and to the protective layer of darkness.

He stops short just before the exit doors, turning to face her, close enough to embrace, and again, his scent makes her want to press her lips to his neck.

Tell me what to do, Joanna. I'm smitten.

There must be something I can do to make this right.

I'm married, Joanna says.

He takes a step back, as if smacked.

Punishment enough, he says, shaking his head sadly. *Although, the punishment may exceed the crime.*

He turns to open the back door for her and as she passes she murmurs, *I am sorry.*

Before he can say another word, she makes a beeline to her car, speeding out of the lot as if being chased, his dejection in her rear view mirror.

Mission accomplished, she thinks, with no satisfaction whatsoever. In fact, she feels the loser. Something she had no idea she needs has slipped through her fingers.

Dan returned home while she was out, and calls, looking for her, surprised she's not there to greet him, he says, when she answers. She tells him she's on her way and when she arrives, mumbles about a drink with a friend, nothing about Loren's lovelorn tale or the plot to avenge. She can see he will not much care. He's excited about a new project.

Might be more time away, he says, *but if it goes as well as hoped, the last. Six months, maybe. Too interesting to turn down, Jo. I'll tell you more in the morning. I have a few notes yet for the write-up. And I'm beat.*

He is not asking for her approval, or her interest, for that matter, and nothing she will say will deter him. He has what he needs.

Loren calls a few days later to say she's back in the saddle and has had a lovely video visit with a charming man.

Joanna, however, lays awake late into the night, and mopes through her days. The assignation with Jason lingers in her mind. She wants to see him again. She wants to talk to him about all sorts of things. She longs to feel the warmth of his touch. Much as she tries to regain a semblance of reason, she cannot dispel an inexplicable sense of grief.

One morning, a week later, at the first hint of dawn, Dan sleeping peacefully beside her and his bag packed by the door for the next trip, Joanna slips out of bed and down the hall to the den. She locates Jason's phone number and sends a message.

I'm sure you're familiar with the Kalash people in northern Pakistan, she texts, as if merely continuing a conversation. *Women choose their mate, and if that man does not keep her happy, he can be discarded.*

Within moments, as if he's been waiting for her, he replies. *As I recall, a woman is free to choose another, if she wishes.*

Joanna sighs contentedly. *That tribe also believes in forest fairies who match up the unattached, or women with wandering husbands.*

A good woman deserves better, he replies. *A good woman deserves attention.*

She can picture his smile.

Suffering is Optional

To the front of the chapel, facing the slightly raised pulpit, Ron's family has coalesced to the left of the aisle, an exact duplicate of how they lined up at the wedding twenty-two years ago. His elder sister and her husband, and their middle-aged son and daughter, their spouses having made their apologies, flew in just hours ago from Seattle, and his younger brother from Toronto, Canada, where Ron and his siblings were raised, with his two sons, one with his partner, the other with his current wife, and his ex-wife, mother of the two boys, still a friend to Janey. Clustered close, nearly inanimate, as if they had stumbled in error into the chapel, they murmur conspiratorially, glancing now and then behind them in search of mourners they might recognize, and watching for Janey to take her seat, growing restless, like everyone else, to get on with the memorial program, so they might get on with grieving.

In the rows behind them, nearly filled,

escorted to their place by one of Janey's friends serving as ushers, an assemblage of husbands, colleagues, friends, neighbors, and a handful of longstanding merchants, lined up like gawky adolescent boys at a dance.

When was the last time we were in a church? one whispers, loud enough to be heard without disrespecting the solemnity.

The university chapel, not a church, his immediate neighbor corrects.

Weddings, funerals, that's it these days, another says. *Getting weird.*

Getting old, the one on the end leans over to chime in. *Ron, I suppose, planned this.*

I'm sure the university was pleased to host, he's a distinguished alum.

He had plenty of time to plan.

And Janey would do what he asked her to do.

They all nod. Despite Ron's embrace of the present, his unfathomable comfort with the unknowable, they are certain he orchestrated his finale, Janey, his devoted spouse, and the executor, facilitating his every wish.

On the other side of the aisle sits a packed row of roughly thirty elder women Ron called the gal pals – a network as cohesive and ionized as an electric circuit. They sit atypically inert, like chess pieces at the open, wearing tasteful dresses, exposing little or no cleavage, hems below the knee, mostly black or gray, an occasional navy. Here and there, a lightweight cardigan, as cool air has coasted into fall on the fog shrouding coastal northern California.

Ron once likened these women to the southern desert wildflowers which erupt after winter rains: graceful stems rising exuberantly from sandy earth by virtue of stylishly cut hair in luminous shades, blonde or brunette. From Janey's vantage point, at the doorway to the chapel, their gold or auburn highlights mimic the bolts of color radiating through the stain-glassed windows.

She stands at attention at the top of the steps leading to the chapel, expectation etched onto her gently lined face. She could easily be mistaken for a hostess at a restaurant checking reservations. Unsteady on high heels, her feet are already sore. She's determined however to present with grace. To soar above her petite frame and the tension of this day and all that has come before. By way of greeting, she nods, appreciably. She leans in for a hug or a kiss, on one cheek, or both. She presses a palm over her heart now and then, in response to kind words.

She holds a program coiled into a tube, as if she might swat away a bug. Her stomach churns, a stuffed sack of fruit that might suddenly tear, scattering haphazardly to the ground.

As she awaits the latecomers, her eyes are drawn to dust motes trapped in ribbons of light hanging from the chapel's vaulted ceiling, uncertain whether they float up to the heavens or down toward the redwood floor. Rising or falling between the ethereal and earthly, like Ron, she thinks, an image that makes her smile, but which she instantly banishes to reframe the proper gravitas.

All at once, a cloud blocks the sun, the motes scatter, and Janey wonders if the years with Ron have been an illusion – a reverie from which she will reawaken to the mid-life bride she was, the days and nights between then and now, illusory.

Ron has lost a lifelong battle for life. Death his reward. Perhaps hers, as well.

Most of the guests have arrived, most are seated, embedded in a hush, anticipating formalities as stoney as the huge rectangular plinth in front of the pulpit on which a casket is meant to rest; instead, the antique brass urn containing Ron's ashes, like an ancient artifact, made more ceremonial by the empty space surrounding it.

The gal pals wanted to rim the urn with vases of fresh flowers from their gardens, as if sentries to the next life, but Janey insisted, as Ron had, on austerity.

She has been touched by the attendance of the next generation, the adult children of friends or family. *How sweet of you to make time,* she tells each one as they arrive.

Ron was like an uncle, they say. *A huge influence on my life. I can't believe he's gone,* they whimper, tears dripping from their eyes.

Loss will become increasingly, painfully present for the young, she thinks. For elders, just another click of the clock.

She graciously welcomes the stragglers, hoping by greeting them now she might avoid the more emotional farewells after the service, the tears, the sorrow, rising to the surface when resistance has been worn down.

So kind of you to come, she murmurs, like a mantra, as she has for an hour or more, in awe of the magnitude of the crowd, far beyond expected. She's glad now Ron requested this chapel, as neither were members of a tribe. A large, bright space, soaring ceilings and elegant windows, without religious symbolism. The indifferent and the observant equally welcome.

She wears a charcoal gray knit dress she purchased last year for the occasion. Ron urged her to buy several and model them, not for his approval, rather his appreciation.

Don't wear black, was his one request. *Western culture. Wear white, the eastern tradition.*

No way, Janey argued. *I'll look like a ghost and they'll all think I've gone mad.*

They know you too well, and they know me. They'll understand. Better yet, wear purple, like widows in Thailand. Purple suits you.

The purple dress hangs in the closet, the tag still on it. This one request, denied.

When she brought home a selection of dresses, she dug out stiletto heels tucked high on a shelf and pretended to sashay a catwalk. Ron applauded each dress with salacious glee. Pitch black, smokey black, charcoal, espresso, the deep purple saved for last, which he slowly peeled from her body, then removed the heels, one by one, taking his time to please her, before they watched the sunset from bed, as if just another day, rather than approaching the last.

Memory is not a tonic, she thinks, as she stands at the chapel door. More like a well in which she might plummet if she's not mindful. She pulls her shoulders back, straightens her spine, standing tall, as if invincible, then runs fingers through her short sandy hair, purple strands at the crown in honor of her husband.

Her sister, Susan, serving as lieutenant, has urged everyone to sign the guest book and note their connection, although Janey knows them all, because, as Susan reminded her this morning, like on their wedding day, and other special occasions, details blur. To Janey's mind, today, perhaps, a blessing.

Everyone has a program in hand with Ron's picture on the front, and beneath this, a favorite quote from Walt Whitman he chose.

Every atom belonging to me as good belongs to you.

The pre-printed thank you notes feature the same quote. The house has been prepped for visitors. Janey has deftly curated the few speakers, and she's organized the proceedings to meet Ron's stipulations.

Too late now to interrogate what she might have missed. She's kept most, if not all her promises.

Ashes to ashes, someone will surely say, although it's impossible to imagine any human being as vitally important to their lives charred to ash. Janey has also been instructed where the ashes will be scattered, although she argued, to no avail, for a gravesite or a stone, some sort of physical presence to visit, but Ron lived, and died, determined to be, and then be gone.

Looks like they're all here now, Susan says.

Go ahead and sit, I'll be there soon, Janey answers, pressing a palm to her sister's cheek because she knows her heart is aching, she the woman Ron called his other wife.

As Susan makes her way to her seat in the front pew, Janey gazes again over the large crowd. Even from a distance, from behind, she can identify everyone, each a distinctly defined silhouette, a way of holding their heads higher or lower, the slump or square of shoulders, those who tend to shrink from the crowd or those with a singular and compelling aura, as Ron would say.

None more than the women – a modern version of the wailing widows of ancient times – Janey's support network and Ron's reward.

Her hiking group fills the first row: ten women who have traveled as a pack for thirty years, proudly sustaining strides into their sixties. Twice a year, they take off for several days. From Big Sur to Sedona, or the golden glow of Aspen, they choose a modern cabin or a ski lodge, sufficient space to ensure adequate sleeping areas and, a top priority, a large well-appointed kitchen, because after a full day of hiking, after showers and checking in with loved ones or colleagues, the women prepare a communal meal, sipping wine start to finish, relishing the grand setting, the euphoria of somatic stimulation, and liberation from their obligations to their children, work, partners or aged parents. From trailheads to hillsides, and on to steeper slopes, they rise, like a flock of birds in formation, exalting in the restorative atmosphere.

The most recent trip was to Tahoe, the view above the lake, they said, was majestic. Janey passed on the trip, only the second time she missed an outing, because Ron's health had deteriorated sufficiently to stay at his side. The group considered canceling altogether, but she insisted they go, without disclosing how close Ron was to his end. When he died, they were still away. She did not call. They would return the next day, and there was nothing they could do, not for him, not for her. Not then. Not now.

Oh, dear one, we're here for you, you're not

alone, said their leader when she arrived, a woman known for platitudes and a huge heart.

But I am alone now, Janey might have said, with neither remorse nor despair.

The book group sits behind them. Three SUV's full came together, although, as a rule, only eight attend the monthly meeting, at one or another's home, where they enjoy a potluck meal and literary discussion, if they like the novel, and if not, when they think the story too abstract, or disturbing, or cannot sympathize with the characters, they share photos from recent travels, or their grandchildren, and then agree to the next title before calling it a night, the pleasure of their longstanding camaraderie more meaningful than words on a page.

The political action group also arrived together. *This too shall pass,* the group's founder said. She has snow white hair, face lined like a blueprint, and tired eyes: a woman who shows up first for friends in need, and steps up to make the decisions otherwise daunting in the midst of a crisis.

Janey nodded, swallowing the laughter suddenly rumbling to her lips, as if she had been plopped onto the stage of an absurdist comedy. This will pass sooner than you think, she might have said.

A few of the older women have already lost loving partners. Others have shed spouses, or been shed. Some wear their solo status like a badge of honor, others like a dead weight on their backs. In contrast to younger members, their funeral attire is out of fashion and worn perhaps too often. Janey joined the group in 2017, just after the nationwide women's march. As a rule, she avoids politics. She despises fear mongering and incendiary rhetoric. However, she is alarmed by vast inequities, particularly access to quality health care. Ron, fortunately, had excellent coverage, which he ensured for all his employees, and the care of practitioners who respected his beliefs and made it possible for him to live longer than even he expected. Since the opiate diaspora, and the Covid fiasco, Janey has put her trust only in naturopaths and nurses, and has dedicated a great deal of time to sponsoring pro-healthcare politicians, with Ron's endorsement and financial support.

She checks her watch, impatient now, although the service is on schedule. She awaits only the Buddhist monk Ron asked long ago to speak at his memorial.

People will expect words. Ritual. They will

want to honor my passing, he told her. *And they will seek closure, although we know there is no closure, only acceptance.*

Janey nodded at the time, willing to adopt her husband's wisdom as her own. Now, she wonders. Closure, acceptance, these are on a generally accepted continuum of grief. What she faces ahead, although she may not conform to the pattern, but what does it matter?

The air has warmed, the sun rising in a clear blue sky, as if to sanctify the proceedings, and into its glow, the monk appears before her. Wrapped in a golden robe, his bald, browned head shimmers, as if oiled. His round face is free of blemishes or wrinkles, limpid eyes like tidepools, and he smells of patchouli.

Amituofo, he says to Janey: an expression of greeting, as well as good wishes.

She nods, as she was coached, folding both hands to her heart to mirror his.

When she leads him into the chapel, he follows slowly, as she makes her way down the aisle to the first pew, where a seat next to hers has been saved for him. He, however, does not stop, continuing to the altar, and parks himself to one side of the plinth, where everyone can see him. They all stare at him, like a meditative focal point, as he gazes before him with an otherworldly expression. In the solemnity of his presence, the crowd breathes easily. No less sad, but reassured the service will commence. Ron's life will at last be celebrated.

Janey is not a Buddhist. She learned the essential ideology and terms, and the gestures, from Ron, who was struck dumb as a freshman in college by an appearance by the Dalai Lama. He told her he had yet to encounter anyone who embodied peacefulness, a way of being he determined then to replicate, navigating his life's journey with neither an allegorical nor physical cane.

Ron's sister told Janey that even when a young child, he was spookily mindful. *He won all the staring games,* she said, her laughter tinged with resentment. His mother told her she could have left the house for hours and Ron might not have noticed. He was typically and totally absorbed by tinkering, from play dough to building blocks and magnetic tiles, and on to Legos, he progressed to circuitry, and pursued an undergraduate degree in cognitive science, which he described as the delicate blending of philosophy and physics. He wrote a thesis on transforming the tangible into the intangible, refuting the prevailing theory of the reverse, which led him to UC Berkeley for a PhD.

Ron tinkered not for the sake of what he might construct or create, rather the pleasure of immersion, and then tinkering turned into a career devising technology triggers to augment medical research. He sold first one just before he met Janey, then a highly prized version 2.0, retaining the patents, which made him a small fortune, and, rather than retire, he founded a think tank of similarly eccentric tinkerers he branded Tin, in honor of the iconic *Wizard of Oz* Tin Man, extolled as a *good-deed doer*.

In contemporary parlance, he was the personification of presence. Nothing like the husbands who measured their worth only in the tangible. Ron worked as much and as long as he had to, until he no longer wanted to, and then anointed a similarly principled CEO, then serving as mentor and advisor since.

He was sixteen when he was diagnosed with kidney disease, which he insisted was a blessing more than a curse. *Knowing one's life is short, not limited, albeit constrained, is a path to a fuller life. Fragility is a source of strength. Outlook, not time, defines us.*

He explained to Janey on their first date,

his medical condition was parenthetical. *Pain is inevitable, suffering is optional,* he said, a Buddhist truth he adhered to until his last breath.

Are they not the same? Janey asked.

One would think, yes, but not quite. Pain, struggle, these are integral to living. They cannot be ignored, or deleted. How we respond, how we live with pain, this is what defines us, Ron answered.

At an annual silent retreat, he mastered transcendental meditation and he learned to elevate himself into a spiritual state known as Samadhi: a stillness in which mind and body detach from all else. Janey would occasionally come into the den and find him in what she likened to a catatonic state, and she would wait, anxiously, until his eyes flickered open and he smiled, a smile, she told friends, that elevated his being beyond his reality.

The last time he was able to evaporate, as he preferred to say, she found him sitting shockingly still on his meditation cushion, his breathing undetectable, the subtle vibration of a throw blanket wrapped around his shoulders the only sign he was more than an apparition. At last, she cried out with exasperation, *Ron!*

He nodded, ever so slightly, opened his

eyes and said, *I'm calibrating the wind.*

At moments like those, Janey wanted to beat her fists into his chest, or grab him by the shoulders to shake him into a shared reality. Treat him as if he were an ordinary human. But he was not. There was no one like him, and whoever loved him had to love and accept him, vulnerability and eccentricity at once.

He was thirty when his second kidney failed and a transplant had to do the work of two since. The miracle, Janey called the aged organ that lasted far beyond its shelf life. To her mind, a matter of mind over matter.

To Ron's mind, Janey was the miracle. The balance he had been seeking and the joy he had been missing.

From the first, they made the most of all they had. They hiked the ancient Camino from France to Spain. The stood in awe at the feet of the Chinese terracotta soldiers. They wandered remains of the Greek city of Ephesus in Turkey. On the rare occasions Ron wished to be home for a while, to recharge, he claimed, he dispatched Janey with gal pals on a river cruise down the Rhine or a guided Safari in Tanzania, insisting she take regular respites from the care and feeding of a man becoming less functional.

Even when chronic milkiness veiled his eyes, and his energy frequently flagged, Ron insisted they return to Japan to revisit Kyoto's gardens, and on to Thailand, drifting on a slow boat down the Mekong River to Laos, then to Vietnam to sail the mystical Ha Long Bay.

Soon after their return from that trip, pneumonia compelled a prolonged antibiotic regimen, and then, pernicious anemia turned his skin as pale as parchment.

Covid nearly killed him. Janey managed to avoid the cursed virus and Ron survived, although weakened, and with mounting pain. He walked more slowly. He slept poorly. He bruised easily, purple blotches spreading over his hands and arms like craters on the moon. He joked that in another era he would have been banished to a leper colony.

Again, Janey served as his source of his sanity, also salvation. A former librarian, she spent hours researching every possible proven alternative treatment to keep him going and keep the pain to a minimum.

A year after he was finally sprung from a longer lockdown, and despite the steep hills he knew he would have to climb, he insisted on a pilgrimage to Nepal, and returned with an even more dramatic sense of serenity.

Day by day, however, the man whose spirit seemed to rise above them all, and, by extension, elevated theirs, steadily failed. Janey served as commander in chief, the women her battalion of spare drivers or shoppers, and her companions during his longer hospital stays. They kept her well fed and poured her wine when her resilience wilted, and stocked the kitchen with an abundance of nourishing foods for Ron's return.

The Jewesses cooked chicken soup they called nature's penicillin. The Asians, curries, overflowing, they claimed, with antioxidants. Latinas offered pots of chili to warm body and spirit. One hiker was renowned for sour dough bread, which Ron dipped lustily into a garlicky hummus another delivered. A team of bakers presented still warm pies or brownies, because Ron had a sweet tooth.

No matter how weak, or the depth of his pain, he treasured their good cheer nearly as much as they cherished his affection. One of a kind, they all said. The sweetest apple on a tree of flawed fruit.

Perhaps the gods, the spirits, whatever faith or ideology, would protect a man like this, they hoped, even as he grew weaker. Janey too began to harbor a fantasy he would defy the odds, despite increasingly frequent middle of the night sweats, muscle spasms so severe only a CBD rub and cannabis eased his agony, and then, a failing libido, even with a blue pill.

Insult to injury, he carped.

When, at last, at Janey's urging, he capitulated to narcotic painkillers, he said they made him feel like a zombie, and he marched stiffly about the house, his arms held straight out and a maniacal expression on his face, to make her laugh.

The crushing blow came when he was unable to focus sufficiently to meditate. That was the day Janey knew the end was near.

To the people in the pews awaiting the memorial, his passing was as devastating as inevitable. For Janey, the same, and, as well, an unexpected overwhelming relief she could not and would never disclose.

You must be an angel, because only an angel can live with a heavenly creature, Ron's sister said, long ago, which Janey assumed then the griping of a grumpy sibling.

Recalling her words today, Janey would say, yes, true, impossible to live with a saint. In truth, she never believed she deserved him, and the burden of living up to someone so far above most mortals proved as exhausting as his care. She fluctuated between the fear of losing him and wishing they had never met. She would never have admitted to anyone, not even her sister, certainly not deifying friends, a question nagging her many years: if Ron were healthy, what sort of man might he have been? Would she have loved him the same?

Suffering is optional, Janey murmured to herself, as she sat in her place in the chapel. Then again, she would say, stoicism is merely a matter of fortitude.

Ron's brother gave the formal eulogy, eliciting many nods, a spattering of laughs, a few tears. The CEO of Tin spoke on behalf of his colleagues and the Dean of the School of Sciences honored his achievements.

Ron's sister recited a short poem.

By David Harkins, she read.

You can shed tears that he is gone. Or you can smile because he has lived. You can close your eyes and pray that he will come back, or you can open your eyes and see all that he has left. Your heart can be empty because you can't see him. Or you can be full of the love that you shared.

They all nodded as one, orchestrated, in effect, and then, a hush descended over the crowd, as the monk seemed to glide into place at the plinth. He gazed at the urn for a moment, or two, which seemed eternity to the mourners, before he faced them to speak, his voice like spring water on a summer day.

I am not here to exalt, that is not my intent. Ron knew this. No need for praise.

Like Caesar, Susan thought, hailing her beloved brother-in-law.

Like Jesus, Ron's sister thought, as if her brother might have walked on water if he'd put his mind to it.

The monk went on to paraphrase the *Tibetan Book of the Dead.*

Ron died a good and peaceful death. And through the triumph of his death, he will benefit all other beings, living and dead.

The crowd nodded again, all harboring a similar thought: Ron was sick most of his life, he dealt with it gracefully and died the same. End of story.

The monk closed his eyes, and chanted for a time in Sanskrit.

You may chant with me, he invited the mourners as he opened his eyes and smiled the smile of those who seem to know what mortal beings never learn.

I take refuge in the Buddha. I take refuge in the Dharma. I take refuge in the Sangha, he intoned, encouraging mourners to join him.

The crowd murmured, then bellowed in response, relenting to the cadence, inspired by his words, without comprehension, the way parishioners in a church, a temple or a mosque, are moved merely by the resonance of prayer.

A musician from the monastery, also in a robe, who had entered the chapel silently and waited at the back for his cue, floated toward the plinth. He cradled a lute and, with a bow to the monk, and then to the mourners, he began to strum, the tone beatific and exultant.

Go in peace, dear friend Ron, the monk concluded at the close.

The mourners murmured the same, as many wept.

Janey heaved a great sigh, which those near her assumed to be grief, rather than the resound of a boulder being catapulted from her path. She will no longer stand at the base of the Sisyphean hill, she thought. Whatever the pain, she will not suffer another moment.

At the reception line, where Janey and

the family stood to receive the attending, the university chaplain, who stood at back during the service, took Janey's hand and whispered the words of Rilke.

Death is our friend precisely because it brings us into absolute and passionate presence with all that is here, that is natural, that is love. You will meet him again in heaven, he added.

Janey nodded, but oh so tired of the talk. There is no heaven, she might have cried. There is only this one life to make what you can of it.

Much of the crowd made their way to the cottage Ron had purchased thirty years ago and expanded to add space for Janey when she moved in. Glass doors along the back face the Diablo mountains, where sunlight shepherds the day, and the opposite face the grand San Francisco Bay, where the sky goes pink at dusk.

His haven, their sanctuary, now hers.

Radiating from a portable speaker on the living room fireplace mantle, next to the urn presiding over the mourners, the soulful strains of Nepalese chants from a playlist Ron created for the occasion.

The hiking group presented platters of sandwiches and bowls of salads. Their favorite grocer sent still warm breads with cheeses. The book group displayed an assortment of sweets, much of which would end up wrapped in foil and frozen for the future. The political action group had delivered two cases of wines, stayed a brief time, and then fled, every loss triggering the sorrow of those that have come before.

Suffering is optional, Janey murmured.

Ron's family huddled together, like refugees, making polite conversation until they too fled, promising to visit with Janey the next morning, before they return to their homes.

Finally, only the inner circle of women remained to share memories. Shoes and duty shed, they flopped onto couches and chairs, the overflow on the floor, laughter rippling around the living room like a sports stadium wave.

The time Ron said this, the day he did that…

Janey slips down the hall to the powder room to scoop cold water to the back of her neck, as if she's just crossed the finish line at a marathon. When she returns, she stands in the doorway, observing the bouquet of women, nibbling on bites and sweets, and sipping wine, laughing, or heaving great sighs of sadness.

A book group member quoted Tolstoy. *The kinder and the more thoughtful a person is, the more kindness he can find in other people.*

Amen to that, Janey says.

The women turn to her and smile. They assume she has had too much wine, although, they know, sorrow will do that to a woman.

Her friend Catherine, who attracts men like bees to the sweetness, and tires of them as quickly, seems especially bereft. She called Ron her stand-in. They had lunch the first Thursday of each month to discuss the news of the day, and she always managed to condemn men as if Ron were another species.

Darya, whose husband still keeps long hours as a lawyer, frequently obliged Ron's request to bake Baklava, her grandmother's recipe, she said proudly, which she was happy to do, and Ron happy to consume, and her husband happy for the leftovers.

Ellie, whose spouse suffered a cardiac arrest ten years ago, leaving her a wealthy, lonely widow, dubbed Ron her surrogate. *In almost all ways,* she would say, with a wry smile. After pouring another round of wine for the women and brewing chamomile tea for those needing a gentler beverage, she sits on a club chair by the window and weeps.

Janey is inclined to comfort her, but her well has gone dry.

They have all been widowed, in a way, she thinks now. The tangible, intangible.

Evening settles beyond the cottage and sweeps across the front rooms like an autumn wind. The women take this as their cue. Empty wine bottles are packed into a recycling bin, the rest are topped with corks and lined up on the counter, or in the fridge, for the next round of visitors. They rinse the glasses, silverware and plates, towel-dry and nest them into boxes, the clinking a satisfying soundtrack to domestic pursuits. Platters are stored and dining table wiped. Their efforts are more somber than their usual gatherings, but as synchronized as all such moments they have shared over the years.

Janey slips through a door to the garage where she stares at roughly forty storage bins lining one wall, piled nearly to the ceiling, like Legos labeled by color, shape and size, so when Ron took to tinkering, he quickly located what he needed. She inhales a familiar scent of glue, resin and solvents, and the astringent metallic taste in the air emanating from the many boxes of screws, connectors and nails. On the shelves along the back wall, the remnants of his labors, displayed like artifacts at a museum.

Within weeks, once the mourner parade

ends, and whatever remains to be done is done, she will bequeath the bins to a high school metals workshop and the assemblies to Tin for a permanent exhibit in Ron's honor. She will scrub the garage walls and shelves, and add a fresh coat of paint.

When Janey returns to the house, the women are finalizing sleeping arrangements, piling sheets, pillows and blankets on beds and couches like hotel maids. She will not be alone this night, perhaps a few nights, and she feels her heart descending from the scaffolding on which it has been sheltered so long.

Perhaps, tonight, she will sleep through the night. No more attending to Ron waking, gasping for breath or moaning in pain. No more the rush to an emergency room or worse, the fear she might awaken to a cadaver.

No more the warmth of her husband's affection. No serenity to ground her. No one to welcome her home or urge her on.

Can she make peace with ambivalence? Will she endure the pain without suffering?

She sways some on her feet. Her eyelids grow heavy. Without a word, she goes to her bedroom, closes the door, slips off her clothes, and slides under the coverlet, where she sleeps until the first glimmer of light trickles into the room, beckoning, exhorting, taunting Janey to ask the question Ron would never ask – not of himself, nor of her. The one question she will ask every day in the days to come.

To her mind, the one and only question worth asking. *Now what?* she calls to a rising sun, with equal trepidation and elation.

What now?

Where You Are

Gangsta rap, oddly named, a harsh dialect I neither understand nor can abide, booms from my new neighbor's window from mid-morning into evening, although rarely after dark. When I moved to this apartment, just as the pandemic lockdown was winding down, I asked the offender, Mario is his name, to lower the volume. He smiled, a wry smile, paused, then replied, with no hint of contrition, *I could.*

He never has. The noise emanating from his car is worse – loud, indecipherable voices, and a deafening bass, thunder through the air as he blasts to and from his parking spot, like a jackhammer on wheels.

Mario is short and stocky, with a snake tattoo slithering up one arm and an inscrutable insignia branding the back of his thick neck. He struts around this neighborhood of two-story buildings, each with four apartments, as if the mayor. His home, in the shape of a barn and painted barn red, is one of only two single family houses in the area, and the one spot of color among tan and gray facades fading into the distance like the ubiquitous marine layer. I've noticed him converse amiably with other residents, postmen and delivery drivers, and, despite ignoring my reasonable complaint, he nods respectfully when I pass.

These interlocking streets, developed in the 70s, are located on the upside of southern California's Pacific Coast Highway, PCH, it's called, versus oceanside. Like train tracks, the road delineates more than geography, dividing middle and working classes from the better-heeled. Most, maybe all of my neighbors, are service workers, thus not eligible for remote employment, so it is quiet during work hours, which makes the racket from Mario's house all the more grating. They are mostly what is now known as essential workers, which I was, when I was an ICU nurse, although not designated or treated as such then.

The day I viewed this apartment, after previously exploring a dispiriting selection of tiny places fitting my modest budget, I trailed the landlord as she trudged up the steep metal outdoor staircase to the upper level. A short, slight woman, with tightly cropped white hair and rounded shoulders, she wore a loose-fitting tan dress, like a gunny sack, tied at the waist with a narrow belt, more fastidious than fashionable. She was breathing hard by the time she got to the top, where she turned to me and smiled, as if commiserating, and I smiled cordially in return, although I was not winded. My legs, after so many years on my feet, suffer fatigue, often, but still sturdy, and I take brisk walks three times a week to enhance the blood flow. As she entered a four-digit encryption into a keypad mounted to the door, she cupped one hand over the other to prevent me from reading the code, and I had to stifle a laugh. A compact, silver-haired woman, wearing black khaki slacks and a pressed powder blue linen blouse, is hardly the profile of a thief, and my rental application had been already vetted. On the other hand, seniors are urged to protect personal privacy. Better safe than sorry.

The spaces I'd seen before made me fear I'd been priced out of the town where I've lived over thirty years, so I was shocked when she opened the door to reveal a bright spacious apartment. A scent of sawdust and paint, and a noxious layer of ammonia, clotted the air, the place in need of airing, otherwise spotless.

Tall casement windows invite sunlight from room to room all day, with an abundance of recessed lighting to repel the dark hours. Engineered wood floors, tinted a maple tone, abut walls painted a neutral tone reminiscent of sand. I was at first, ironically now, struck by an impression of calm. Mario must have been somewhere else that day.

In the midst of gloom there is a light, I remembered – an adage passed down from my mother and on to my son and daughter, all the more meaningful in that moment.

I still believe this place was a gift, a safe harbor from which to steer the transition from one stage to the next. From a full life to the final years. Pristine and precise, likely inspired by a TV remodeling guru, albeit not at all like the traditional home with a large yard, where my husband and I raised our children, neither the contemporary condo on three levels, to where we downsized and resided four years, which my husband contended, then, by virtue of younger neighbors and lots of stairs, would keep us young.

I silently surveyed the space I already knew would be my new home.

Perfect for one person, the landlord said,

as if I needed convincing.

Perfect for me, I replied, emphatically.

Mature olive trees and graceful western cypresses shade the southern exposure, like a treehouse, and most nights their leaves rustle in the evening breeze, the salve after daylight hours pierced by Mario's raucous playlists.

My downstairs neighbor, Sylvia, not so much a busybody as gregarious, has the scoop on all the neighbors. She delights in holding, and sharing, secrets, and she explained to me, soon after I arrived, that the landlord inherited the building two years ago and her architect son managed the remodel. She said he also built her a garage apartment at what was once her family home, so she might rent the larger house for more income. What is dubbed now, by senescent professionals, *aging in place*, a utilitarian concept, not always feasible, and not always desirable either for those of us who would rather not stay put, as long as we don't have to forfeit too much that matters.

The day after I moved in, a particularly sizzling late summer day, as workmen were repairing the fence between my parking area and Mario's, I watched as he delivered to them frosty cold bottles of beer and sizzling tacos.

Not for the new neighbor, for them. I've since heard him cooing to his son in his yard. The boy, age seven or eight, tends to shout more than speak, and I suspect his tender ears are already damaged by incessantly high decibel levels. I would suggest a hearing test, perhaps whisper to the mom, although I rarely see her. Maybe she tired of the music.

Mario grows weed, you know, on the fringe of his patio. Over there, Sylvia told me one day, pointing to the back of his property and raising her eyebrows with a cagey smile.

Later that day, from my upper vantage point, I peered out to see strips of thick green bushes, shorter and taller, male and female, I suppose. They reminded me of lush hibiscus a former neighbor of mine, recently deceased, cultivated with great care from a spectacular garden of native and flowering plants. She often gifted cuttings to neighbors, their sweet scent and graceful leaves bowing from a vase from week to week.

These days, I purchase a small seasonal bouquet on Fridays at Trader Joe's.

Early fall, the weather hotter and dry, the dreaded fire season in California, Mario hosed down the cannabis roots at sunset, and during winter's evening chill, he erected heat lamps so tall they beamed into my living room like the ominous glare of towering lights above prison gates. Fitting, as even as a modicum of post-pandemic normalcy resumed, elders felt trapped by the persistent threat.

I sold the condo last year when realtors came calling, the bubbling real estate market hard to resist. Truth be told, I wanted out, after burying my husband of forty-five years, and the subsequent isolation of lockdown. I never liked living on three levels stacked like lumber, and similarly precarious, so it seemed. He had urged the move to cash in on the family home once the kids were grown. Stairs turned out to be, as one might have predicted, the enemy of aging joints, and particularly taxing the years he was ill, so I set up for him a hospital bed on the ground level, which made us feel as if we had gone backwards in time to the studio we lived in when we were first married. We didn't mind being on top of each other then.

When it came time to move, however, none of the affordable housing alternatives – a garage flat, a cottage at the back of someone's property, or any version of senior living – appealed to me.

My daughter, to my amazement, invited me to live with her. She lives an hour away, too far, I felt, from my friends, my favorite shops and walking paths. What social workers aptly call touchpoints.

That guest room with bath is rarely used. Very private. We won't bother you much. And you can see the kids more often, she coaxed.

What she did not articulate, but which I understood, was her concern I should not live alone much longer. After all, who will take care of me if I am faced with a dire diagnosis? I've crossed seventy, which seems old to her, less to those of us who follow the obituaries of friends and neighbors, and the famous, who linger into their nineties now. Although I was grateful for her kindness, I bristled at my daughter's offer. I've grown accustomed to passing my days as I please. I do not wish to be dependent. I'm still healthy, beyond age-related pain and stiffness. And, despite the challenges of relocation late in life, I was eager for a change of scene, although clearly naïve to how extreme the change would prove to be.

The grandchildren, however, were hard to resist. From infancy to sports to Sunday brunches, I've been present. When they were younger, we had tea parties. Yes, boys must also participate in tea parties, I admonished my conventional son-in-law. We baked apple pies at Thanksgiving. Sugar cookies at Christmas. We chopped up quirky toppings for pizza or fillings for tacos, and sometimes for fun, we dipped penne, one by one, into freshly cooked marinara sauce. I introduced them to classic films and Greek myths, before they gravitated to graphic novels and superheroes.

More time with them would be precious, I thought, the time so fleeting.

My son also proposed I move closer to him. He lives two states away, so I demurred, at once, but seized the moment to apologize, again, for moving, twice now, from the home he grew up in, an anchor for my children, which I took away from them and for which I feel terrible guilt. My son, so tender-hearted, reiterated his response from the first. *Home is where you are, Mom,* he said, as if a prayer.

I'd like to think that's still true.

My daughter and her adolescent friends once played a cheeky game called, Who'd You Rather? Oh how they cackled, and sometimes they urged me to play along.

Pitt or Clooney? they teased. *Cary Grant*

or Paul Newman?

These days, seniors more often play Where'd You Rather? What an old friend calls existential geography. Where do we fit? What do we need, or not? Can we reorient ourselves at this late stage of life?

Five years ago, I reluctantly retired from nursing – age, arthritic hands, and technology, rendering me obsolete – just in time to nurse my husband to his end. Too many friends have moved away or passed away, and many have forfeited family homes for financial stability. Little is as it was, ambiguity the one and only constant. Existential indeed.

I do believe our memories, and artifacts, go with us, wherever we nest, so, buoyed by that sentiment, and certain I can make a home wherever I am, I moved into my daughter's guest space and made a concerted effort to flow with their stream. Nevertheless, I could not shake feeling like a boarder, and, as it turns out, cohabitating with my son-in-law proved maddening. I'm quite fond of him. He's good-humored, hardworking, and a devoted father. However, he works remotely from a makeshift office off the living area, trundling around all day dressed in a pressed shirt for videos, obscuring sweatpants or pajama pants, and, between obligations to be on screen, shuffling through the house like a convict in chains, speaking seemingly nonstop into the air via earbuds. He nibbles on protein bars and slugs coffee all morning. Midday, he stands before the refrigerator like a somnambulist, searching for something to whet his eccentric appetite, and, maddeningly, he often pitches a miniature basketball into a hoop mounted to the back of his office door, the thumps resounding as if we lived on a construction site.

In hindsight, better than gangsta rap.

After six months, I decided it was best to live on my own after all, which my daughter did not dispute. Despite her good intentions, I think she too realized that a tenant, particularly a mother, upsets the delicate dynamic a family establishes over time.

My son-in-law, however, expressed his concern over the new neighborhood, which he denounced as working class. He suggested I might feel too much an outsider. He feared for my safety, he said, meaning a preponderance of Latinos living there.

I stood my ground. *Aren't we working class?* I argued. *Besides, I like the vibe.*

Yes, I might have said, I would be living in a blockade of buildings in an area where residents extremely different in skin tone and language might make me feel as caged as the condo, not to mention the untenable noise, but I would strike the right balance, I hoped.

Two weeks later, my son-in-law and my teenage grandson, with the help of a muscular neighbor, loaded my residual furnishings and personal belongings into a U-Haul truck, and moved me to the apartment. My daughter and granddaughter did most of the unpacking and stayed until all the boxes were emptied and broken down, housewares I'd ordered shelved, freshly washed towels and clothes placed in the right places, and miscellany in a hall closet. They tossed the boxes down the outer stairs to pack into the recycling bin, then made my new bed with the new pillows and a puffy quilt they presented as a housewarming gift, into which I crumpled soon after they left and slept until Mario's music shattered the silence.

There's a small balcony off the living room, nothing like the large flagstone patio I once enjoyed, with room for a chaise lounge and a small table, where I planned to read late afternoons. That's also the time sea breezes sail up the hill, delivering the scent of the surf to those of us blessed to live close to the ocean, as if we are perpetually on holiday. Invariably, at this precise moment, Mario, who may also sell his marijuana, I'm not sure, lights up, and the skunky smoke rises toward my balcony and further assaults my senses.

I don't care about my neighbor's taste in music or his penchant for dope, I just don't want to hear it or smell it.

Across the street, a single mom, I think, I've never seen a companion, lives with two nearly grown sons. She leaves early morning in green hospital scrubs and does not return until late in the day. Several of these neighbors wear similar hospital uniforms. I should strike up a conversation sometime, we might bond based on experience, although so much has changed in nursing in recent years, I suspect I'm extinct. I don't really miss the work. I do miss feeling useful. The daily destination. I wonder now if it was in the ICU, where I spent 10-hour days, I developed hyper-sensitivity to sound. Every beep and buzz, every drip, every sudden sigh or cry from a patient, requires an immediate response, often a matter of life and death. My cortisol levels are still elevated, a central nervous system forever taut.

My new neighbors, for the most part, speak Spanish. I've been studying the language for years to challenge my aging brain, also to speak with some proficiency when I can visit friends who have migrated below the border to maximize retirement income. However, they spit words too fast for me to follow, and their idiomatic expressions seem code. I would be embarrassed by my pathetic attempt to speak. On weekends, when many of them are outside washing cars or chatting amiably, their kids playing basketball at a hoop on a garage or kicking a soccer ball between goals spaced out on the street, I try to tune into what they say. Even without comprehension, I appreciate the lilt of the language.

When I first moved in, Sylvia asked if I grew up near here.

I grew up in Chicago, in a neighborhood populated by European immigrants, I answered. *What they used to call a melting pot.*

Si, I've heard the term. A little like us in that way, she exclaimed.

I think we both understood that brown migrants never quite melt in. Maybe none of us ever have.

When I was ten years old, a family from India moved in down the street. Dark brown, they dressed in colorful silks, spoke a staccato language, and the pungent smell of unfamiliar spices leached from their kitchens. They were shunned. For the first time, sadly not the last, I was ashamed for my people. How could they be so inhospitable when they should have been welcoming? Migrants of any origin know what it feels like to dwell in the chasm between there and here, then and now. All these years later, my neighbors' language and solidarity keeps me at arm's length. The shoe on another foot.

The younger son across the street, called Jose, is an adorable boy with dark expressive eyes. Nearly black curls flop around his head, he's slight of build, muscles not yet mounded, and he has a jaunty walk that seems to shout, *my whole life is ahead.* My son once displayed a similar winner take all persona. On the other hand, the frontal cortex is far from fully formed at his age. Decisions not often wise. His older brother leaves late afternoons dressed in a crisp white shirt and black pants, with a shiny black vest. His name is Ibrahim. He has a sweet smile and a melodic voice. He crossed the street one day to help me heave a heavy box up the stairs

UPS had left below, and when I thanked him, he nodded politely, promptly returning to his side of the street. Maybe I should have given him a tip, although, I hope, kindness is its own reward. Sylvia told me he's a waiter at a harbor bar, not far from here, one of her own favorite watering holes, which explains why he returns home near midnight weeknights, later on the weekend. His car music announces his arrival – first a distant beat, steadily louder, rivaling Mario's, until he slows and parks, usually below my bedroom. I've grown accustomed to listening for him before I can sleep, like the many nights awaiting my teenage son or daughter to return home. Often, however, he sits in his car for ten or fifteen minutes, an eternity at that late hour, likely checking social media, while the music blares on, and then, like a switch has been flicked, sudden silence, after which the car door slams, the lock beeps, and, like a reverse alarm clock, I sleep.

A few weeks ago, the mom must have been away, Ibrahim too, leaving Jose to invite a posse to party at the apartment, all day, into the night, and half-way toward dawn. I heard no female voices, only bellicose boys with foul mouths. I hoped it was a one-night nuisance, but I ended up sleeping two nights on a tatami mat in a small second bedroom facing the back, where I pay bills, attend the Zoom Spanish class and a book group, also video visits with friends and grandkids.

By the third night, at midnight, my back desperate for relief, I pulled a sweatshirt and sweatpants over a stretched out T-shirt of my husband's I sleep in, slipped into clogs by the door, and walked across the street to petition the boys to lower their voices.

Jose answered the knock. He was taller than he seemed from a distance, so I had to look up to him, when I would rather he had to look up to me. *I'm so sorry, Miss*, he said, with a contrite smile. The sort of smile perfected by the young, and children of color, to defuse condescension or harm.

Behind him, three boys clustered on the couch. I had expected a dozen of them, given the racket. They were bare to the waist, so thin I could count ribs, wearing plaid pajama pants. Lit by the glare of a large screen television, they seemed as innocent as altar boys, even as they shouted nonstop slurs at a reality series that challenges survival.

Take that, mother fucker, they yelled. *Yeah,*

get him. Crush him. You're done, loser! they cried, peppering reactions with hysterical laughter.

Their hostility, rising from their young bodies like smoke from a raging fire, reminded me of sepia-tinged news reels of Fascists on the streets of Germany and Italy a century ago. Frankly, terrifying. When I nodded my thanks, Jose closed the street-facing window, a futile gesture, and as I made my way back to my apartment, I was deeply disturbed, not only by their language, but how this generation is so quickly acclimated to aggression.

Now I sound like a crochety old woman, which my son on a recent video call intimated when I grumbled about Mario's music.

The next night, just after dark, when the yelling and cursing had again risen irritatingly loud, I called for police intervention. A sheriff pulled up soon after, the ominous red spinning light horrifying, I would think, to adolescents, particularly Latinos, and, regretting the call, I watched with trepidation as he entered the apartment. He stayed just a few minutes before returning to his vehicle, waiting, until the boys flew out of the apartment, clutching backpacks and stuffed shopping bags, piling into one car to flee. For two days, I saw them come and go, collecting bags of food and drink. They must have found another party house.

No more noise, not from them.

Ibrahim and the mother returned at week's end, and yesterday, on my way home from a walk, Jose sat on the landing outside his apartment staring at me with a look not of enmity, nor resentment, rather pity, as if I am one of those elders who don't get it. But I do. I get him. He's young, finding his way. He and his compatriots move through their world as if no one else exists, least of all a crabby neighbor. The truth is, he doesn't get me – he doesn't get that as we age, tranquility should be a reward for working and parenting, being good citizens and neighbors, nursing a loved one to death, and then being trapped in a pandemic-induced horror show. I'd tell him so, but I don't want to be the crusty old lady who preaches. I tolerated one of those when I was a child, because my mother said she was a Holocaust survivor. We all had heard those stories, and seen horrific images, to teach us respect for the struggles of those who came before. I'd like the same.

Down the street, opposite Mario's place, two young boys live upstairs with their parents in an apartment that mirrors mine. Sidewalks and parking areas are their yard. I watch them sometimes playing stick ball and running bases from streetlamps to a hydrant at each corner. These boys are also extremely loud. They are called Luis, perhaps age seven, and Mateo, called Mattie, who must be five. Their mother, Elena, so Sylvia told me, works a call center job at the kitchen table and sometimes, she works on the balcony to watch over her children. I hear her call to them to tie their sneakers or beware the cars before they chase a ball into the street. Her tone of voice is soft, tender, as if to compensate for her boys. The loudest voice of all emanates from the dad, Noah, who is tall and brawny, like a fitness coach. When he shoots hoops with his sons, he whoops and hollers with them, and the other day, he affixed Luis to the back of a bicycle, fastened their helmets and took off down the street like a rocket. *Across the universe*, he roared with the excitement of a man who is, at heart, a boy.

I felt their joy. I recall fondly the thrill of roller skating on city streets, the wind in my hair, as we were not required to wear helmets then. A liberated feeling innate to children, or uninhibited parents, like Noah. Being an elder offers few opportunities to experience that sort of thrill, beyond the vicarious. That may be the hardest part of aging.

I was trained in nursing school, and reminded often by supervisors, to maintain a proper distance with patients. What they called a healthy distance. I wonder now what defines the right distance, because distance, seems to me, translates to disconnection, and I cannot help but feel we so badly need to connect.

I visit weekly with a former neighbor, an eighty-eight year old living alone, refusing to move to assisted living. We sit six feet apart, habit still, on her wide front porch, sharing our concerns about the culture and the planet, and crowing over grandchildren. Before I drive home, I cruise the old neighborhood, gazing longingly at the stately trees and well-tended lawns, inhaling jasmine and lavender, and the stillness, before returning to the commotion of where I am now. On these days, particularly, Mario's music crushes my spirit.

I've read they use metallic rock music to coerce political prisoners into submission and I wonder if I might succumb to a noise-induced madness. I'm considering acquiring a gun, it's easy to do, I'm told, to shoot at the teenagers cursing at the top of their lungs or sitting in cars late at night blaring music. I might fire like a sharpshooter from my balcony at Mario, to extinguish his noise. Eliminate the skunk scent. Perhaps I'll ask him where to buy a gun. He looks like a man who knows. What irony that would be.

Shame on me.

Say it aloud, Gwen, my mother used to say, when I made a disaffected or condemning remark. *If you can't say it, you shouldn't think it.*

Truer words were never said. Just because Mario's pants hang off his hips like a hoodlum and he drives like a bank robber in a getaway car, doesn't mean he's a bad seed.

Besides, if I procured a gun and shot at my neighbors, the newspapers would describe me as mentally ill. Liberals would use me as a reason for gun control. The right wing would track me to my immigrant heritage and decry my roots as a threat to the American dream. Will anyone give due consideration to why a perfectly sane, retired nurse, an American-born mother and grandmother, a woman of modest means with good friends and good habits, turned violent?

I guess I'm not crazy enough to test the waters. Not yet.

Last spring I spent a week visiting my son in Austin, Texas, renewing affection for my grandchildren, and enjoying the picturesque hill town where he lives with his lovely wife. When I described my new neighborhood in greater detail, without mentioning the worst of it, he reiterated his offer to resettle me closer to him. *A large aging population here*, he said, as if new friends can be plucked like flowers.

I wish I had the vigor to begin again in a more gentile place, but that ship has sailed. *Home is where I am*, I whisper to myself now and then, like a prayer.

It's October now, more than a year since I moved here. At dusk, I close the windows facing the street and crack open the ones at back to welcome the evening air. I mark the days, and the time of day, by the street sounds. Sunday afternoon, also Monday, Thursday and Friday nights, cheers and jeers resound from televised football games. Saturday nights, the teenagers party, often late. Wednesday nights, a couple who live in the apartment above Jose and Ibrahim, hold a prayer service. I've no idea the denomination. Twenty or so congregants regularly attend to a pastor's oration, followed by synchronized chanting. In conclusion, they always sing the same song, their voices high and exuberant. I've learned the tune now, so I often hum along. At 9:00 PM, like clockwork, they bid farewell. Lots of *be well, god bless*, they call out, as they descend the stairs, followed by the beeping of car fobs, doors slamming, the rev of engines, and then, a diminishing whir as they drive away, leaving behind the chirping of previously suppressed crickets.

Late at night, long after Mario's music has disappeared, I sometimes hear a swelling wind, or the syncopation of raindrops on the roof. I fall asleep to the cautionary plea of a harbor fog horn, punctuated now and then by the soulful whistle of a train on the coastal tracks. A migratory bird sang all summer in the wee hours and songbirds awaken me at dawn.

I cling to these moments as my patients once clung to life.

Tuesday night is the one reliably quiet night. No sports, no party or church service to rouse voices or tempers. Mario seems to be elsewhere these nights, so I don't have to turn up the volume on my television or tune into a podcast to drown out his music. I have also taken to listening to audiobooks – the voice of a skilled narrator good company while folding the laundry or preparing dinner. Sometimes, I listen while curled into the reading chair in the den, so engrossed in the tale that sometimes, like a bedtime story, I am lulled to sleep.

Tonight, as dusk turned to darkness, I lit lamps in each room, before nestling onto the cushy sofa I splurged on for the living room, to watch another episode of one of the British mystery series I favor. The good guys always win and this always buoys my spirits. For one moment, I don't make a move. I listen to what passes for stillness here. Dishes and cutlery cleared from dinner tables. The noisy boys across the street called to a bath. The talking heads on Sylvia's television below. The low murmur of friendly conversation among evening walkers, against the backdrop of a steady stream of traffic on PCH.

These are buffering sounds. Comforting sounds. The hush of night an antidote to the din of days.

It is at this rare moment, I settle into the silence like a warm bath or a comfy bed.

And then, I hear the plaintive barking of a dog who has been left alone too long.

ACKNOWLEDGMENTS

XX to Dana & Julie, Spenser, Aslan,
Christopher, Thomas & Sean

Thanks to the Readers
Chris, Deborah, Diane, Jacques, Marrie & Paul

And the Cheerleaders
Carol, Robyn, Laura, CQ, Lojo, Deb, Vince,
Andrea, Byron, Kevin, Leslie & Andrew, Liz,
Marianna, Roberta, Sandy, Jeff, Brady, Val,
Leah, Linda, Lin, Bev, Brian & Bradley.

For Kindness and Sustenance
Jacques Garnier
Diane Garrett, Diane's Books of Greenwich
Antoine and friends, Moulin Café
Rick, Laguna Beach Cultural Arts Center

Previously Published Stories
Transcendence, first published as *The Violinist*,
Neither With nor Without, as *There and Then*,
both in *The Write Launch*
Where You Are in *Sequestrum*.

ABOUT THE AUTHOR

A former journalist and marketing/
communications professional, Randy Kraft is
a book reviewer, lecturer and writing coach.
She has published three novels and one story
collection, as well as several short stories and
essays in literary publications.
Where You Are is her second story collection.
A member of PEN America and Writers for
Democratic Action, Randy holds an MAW
[master's in writing] an MBA and a BA in
English/Literature.
Born and raised in NYC, she resides in
southern California.

Info and Contact: www.randykraftwriter.com

Book Reviews: ocbookblog.substack.com

*Anyone who keeps the ability to see beauty,
never grows old.*

Franz Kafka

www.ingramcontent.com/pod-product-compliance
Lightning Source LLC
Chambersburg PA
CBHW061012120726
47910CB00006B/1888